MISSING IN PORTLAND

WRITTEN BY
C. L KENNY

C. L Kenny

Copyright © 2021

By C. L Kenny

C. L Kenny Publications

The characters in this book are purely fictitious. Any likeness to persons living or dead is purely coincidental. However, the author has taken inspiration from the real-life serial killer, David Parker Ray (The Toybox Killer) Some quotes have been directly taken from the tape transcript of David Parker Ray. (YouTube)

For information contact:

https://clkenny.wixsite.com/clkenny
facebook.com/CL-kenny-100487098794059

Don't Forget To Sign Up For The Authors Page!

For special offers, giveaways, bonus content and updates from the author on new releases!

https://clkenny.wixite.com/clkenny
facebook.com/CL-kenny-100487098794059

For Donna…

'When you lose someone you love, you gain an angel that you know.' (2018) C. M Owens

(2021) R.I.P Ladybugs!

CHAPTER ONE

One last check to ensure everything was in order and ready for his next toy.

His workbench was laid out perfectly, with sharpened saws and knives, and the latest penetration machine he had made was all ready. He was looking forward to trying this baby out for the first time.

What a lucky girl she will be.

Gently, he stroked the selection of surgical tools that were lined up neatly. The feel of them under his fingertips was a sensation unlike any other, the coolness of the instrument, the satisfying thought of that very first cut into a fresh piece of meat sending shivers down his spine. They were a part of him, much like his soul. If he still had one. At this, a grin spread across his face.

Unwrapping the packaging from the rope he had purchased, he placed it beside the crocodile clips and blowtorch.

The excitement was building now with the anticipation of the take, reminding him of the feeling children get on Christmas eve. Knowing all good things were soon coming.

Taking the leg spreaders off his gynaecologist chair, he checked the straps were still attached tightly to the stirrups, then sat down and looked around his playpen.

On one side of the room, images of his past playthings decorated the wall. His previous toys in various BDSM positions tied and gagged.

On the other side of the room was a floor to the ceiling rack, holding a variety of whips and dildos in various sizes. Some with nails poking out at the ends, some with razor blades sticking from the sides, all with the purpose of ripping and shredding.

None for pleasure, except for his own.

He just needed to get a new tape for the video recorder that was facing the chair, and all was ready.

Looking up, he winked at himself in the mirror. He really loved this part…

***

"Missing! Fourth woman missing in three months! The Portland Police Bureau has today announced they have received reports of a fourth woman missing in the city of Portland," Mallory read aloud as she took another bite of her toast. "Despite extensive inquiries, and many reported sightings, the women are yet to be found. Family desperate for answers." Looking up from the newspaper article, "When is this going to happen to me?"

"Why do you want to go missing?" her father asked her with a raised eyebrow.

"Not missing, silly," she said between chews. "When am I going to get a big story like this? I need a big, juicy break, or I'm still going to be living with you when I've got gray hair too. And I'm sure neither one of us wants that!" she said, smiling behind her coffee cup.

"Well, I don't know about that. I've kind of got used to you being around," he said as he walked to the counter, pouring himself another coffee. William raised the pot, silently offering Mallory a refill.

"Seriously, Dad! Nothing ever happens here," shaking her head at his invitation. "It's all clearly happening in Portland!" Groaning, she tucked a long strand of dark hair behind her ear.

"I'm sure something will come up soon, Mally."

"I can't sponge off you forever! I need money, I need to save, I need to move out. But more importantly, I need the new Urban Decay color palette they have just released! And there's no way I can justify that at the moment." She looked miserably at her father, who had begun belly laughing at her first world problems.

"Oh, Mally! Don't you have enough make-up?"

"No, Daddy. It's the new Metallics!"

Watching her still handsome father chuckling at her all over again, she picked up another piece of her breakfast.

"Give yourself a break, Mal. You've not long left college, and you've already had a few articles printed."

"Yes, but I'm ready to write something gripping now. An article that no newspaper could resist buying. Not write another article on missing cats or what the local church is doing for their next fundraiser." Since earning her Bachelor's degree in Journalism, she was eager to make a name for herself.

"Where did you say this was happening? Portland?" he asked, sipping at his coffee. His green-olive eyes which matched her own, still laughing at her.

"Uh, huh." she nodded, looking back down at the article.

"Let me make a phone call."

"What? To who?" Mallory's head whipped up from the newspaper.

"You remember my ole buddy Thomas Riley, don't you?" he asked, fishing for his phone from his pants pocket.

"Mm, I think so…" Frowning, she tried to remember. Her father had lots of friends; everyone who knew him well liked him.

"Well, he owns a ranch up in Oregon… Amity," he explained while typing on his phone, "That isn't far from Portland." Mallory looked on excitedly as William lifted the phone to his ear.

She could hear the ring tone suddenly stop as an answering machine kicked in.

"Hey Tom, it's Will. Thought I'd call you; it's been a while! I know you're probably knee deep in horse shit at the moment, so call me back once you've washed your hands. Got a favor to ask." Ending the call and putting his phone back in his pocket, he looked back to Mallory. His face crinkling as he smiled.

"You would probably remember his boys more than Tommy himself. When you were little, you wouldn't leave his oldest alone. Neil... no... no, Noah! He was five or six years older than you. I don't think he appreciated you following him around like you did..."

"Ha-ha, how old was I?"

"Around ten."

Ten.

That had been her age when her mother had left them. Packed up her things. No goodbye, no explanation, just a message to say she wasn't happy anymore, she was leaving, and then gone... Never to be seen by either of them again. Phone number changed, no visits, no cards or birthday calls. No Christmas presents or graduation gifts. Nothing. Nada.

"... In the Marines now,"

"Huh?" Shaking her thoughts off from her mother and giving her full attention back to her father.

"Noah? He's a military man now."

"Ooh!" She nodded.

"I'm sure Tom and his wife Susan, would love for you to go for a visit."

"Really?"

"I'm certain of it. They are forever asking me to visit with them for a riding holiday, so I'm sure they would be more than happy for you to stay with them for a while. See if you can dig up something for our local rag."

"Well, it would certainly be a lot more interesting than what's been happening around here recently and worst-case scenario, it would be great to get in the saddle again." Mallory really missed riding. Her mother had been a big fan of horses;

she had taught Mallory to ride not long after she had learned to walk. But college life and studying had made it difficult.

Standing up and downing the rest of his coffee, William walked over to their open-plan kitchen and put his cup in the sink. He reached down for his briefcase and looked at the watch Mallory had gifted him for his fiftieth birthday.

"I'll be home around six. Maybe you should think about starting your day too," he said with a grin, looking at Mallory still in her pajamas.

"Yeah, yeah… Chilli okay for dinner? I need to go to the store later, so let me know if you need anything."

"Thanks, Mally, but I'm all good."

He smiled as he saluted her, whistling as he picked up his keys from the hook next to the front door. "Be good," he called as he left the house.

"You too."

She looked out of the patio doors that faced their small, but tidy backyard. Mallory lifted her arms and stretched. It was going to be another hot day, and it wasn't even summer yet. Her mind went back to the possibility of Amity for a few weeks. She smiled. Mountains, lakes, and horses. Perfect! And how great it would be if she came home with a story to support her research and help build her portfolio.

She scraped her chair back and picked up the remnants of their breakfast.

Thomas and Susan Riley. Straining to remember, she was certain she remembered Susan, a lovely woman who always had a dog or two by her feet, and then the boys. She was sure there were three of them.

Noah, like her dad had mentioned, who Mallory had remembered having a bit of a young-girl crush on, was older than her and would let Mallory play on his computer console. She smiled. That was probably why she had liked him. When romance was simple!

Next, she was pretty sure, was Aiden, a fiery-red-haired boy with freckles, and the same age as Mallory… She remembered him not being so friendly to her. In fact, thinking about it now, she was sure he had been quite cruel to her, not wanting to take turns playing on the computer with Mallory, 'girls are trash at computers.' Groaning at the memory, she filled the dishwasher before switching it on.

And then there was the little one… Kyle… no Cole. He must have been around six when she had last seen him. He was a real cutie, with crazy, curly, blond hair and big chubby cheeks. She smiled again, wondering what they were like now. Hopefully, she would get the chance to find out soon.

Walking into her bathroom and turning on the shower, she groaned in pleasure as the hot stream of water hit her skin. Reaching for the body wash bottle, she lathered her arms with the sweet scent of vanilla, inspecting her tattoos as she washed. Mallory was a big fan of body art. She had both of her sleeves decorated, one arm with books and symbols of her favorite novels, while the other was full of sugar-skull designs. Big, bold, and full of color, which suited her personality perfectly.

Switching off the water, she reached for her fluffy towel, her mind wandering back to the newspaper article and the missing women. The paper had said the girls were between the ages of seventeen and twenty-two.

Alison Kelly was the first to disappear three months ago, Mallory was sure she was nineteen. Followed by Phoebe O'Neil, six weeks later. She was twenty-two and the oldest of the missing women, she had stuck out the most for Mallory because she was the mother of a six-month-old baby boy. Phoebe's parents had been looking after her son the day she had gone missing, and there had been a lot of speculation on whether Phoebe had disappeared, or rather, couldn't cope with motherhood and simply ran away, abandoning her new baby with her parents, something they had both strongly refuted, stating their daughter loved her son and she was thriving at being a new mother, and it wasn't even a possibility she would have left him deliberately.

The next to go missing was Harriet.... Mallory squinted, racking her mind... Harriet Dolan. She was the youngest to have gone missing at only seventeen, and was reported missing only three weeks after Phoebe. She was a lover of horses and had gone riding the day she hadn't come home.

The latest missing girl was a twenty-year-old Leilah Wyatt, and the image of her innocent face from the newspaper article flashed in Mallory's mind. This girl had seemed different from the rest, but Mallory couldn't pinpoint what it was... Then it hit suddenly her! Leilah was the only girl not to have dark hair! In fact, she had been the only one to have long, blonde hair.

Wondering if she were onto something, Mallory opened her wardrobe and assessed her clothes, searching for the khaki green top she had already planned on wearing, wondering if it would pair better with her black jeans, or her light gold, baggy trousers... Definitely the latter she decided. With her dark green Doc Martens, that would look cute.

She always looked her best, no matter what she was doing or where she was going. Perhaps this was an effect of her mother abandoning her at such a young age, never feeling like she was good enough. She couldn't help but think maybe her mother would have stayed if she had been the perfect little girl.

Not wanting to start her day off with negative thoughts of her mom, she forced herself to think about this morning's breakfast conversation instead. She was in a beneficial situation with living at home with her father still, able to drop everything and travel hundreds of miles away, follow a story she could really get her teeth into, and support her research into the reasons people go missing.

She was really hoping her dad's old college buddy and his wife would be happy for her to stay for a few weeks, so she could try and figure out what the hell was happening in Portland. Why and how these women were disappearing like flies!

Organizing the rest of her pretty boring day out in her head, she made a mental note to check her bank balance. Maybe she could stretch to buying that new Urban Decay color palette after all…

CHAPTER TWO

After securing all the locks, he let out a long, satisfied breath.

This was the most exciting stage. He was just like a kid with a new toy.

If people realized how much fun it was to keep a sex slave, then half of the women in America would be chained up in someone's basement. He let a small chuckle out.

He was excited to return. She would be used hard, especially during the first few days. While she was still new and fresh.

This one was a beggar. She was already offering him money and even sex if he cut her loose. Why she offered sex, he didn't know. She was his for the taking.

But his chained captives would say anything for him to cut them loose. Some threatened, some begged, some even lied. But none of it ever worked. It always led to their demise.

If they were worth taking, then they were worth keeping... if only for a little while.

His favorite toys were those who waited for an opportunity to escape. They were the ones who still held a glimmer of hope in their eyes.

He liked to keep them around for longer.

***

With tears streaming down her face, Mallory opened the kitchen window, stuck her head out, and drew in a deep breath. Damn! she hated chopping onions.

The sun was setting, and the sky had turned a beautiful shade of pink. It looked so pretty and picturesque tonight.

Taking another breath, she pulled her head back in and wiped under her eyes.

Facing the oven again, she ignited the hob, waited a moment for the pan to heat, before adding in the evil smelling onions. She began singing softly along with the radio, giving the pan a stir, before adding more ingredients.

Knowing her father would be home soon, she took two wine glasses out from the cupboard and walked over to the wine rack. Picking out a nice Pinot, she was about to open the bottle when the front door opened and her father walked in.

"Hey, Mally. I'm home."

"Hey Dad, how was your day?" she asked, while pouring them each a glass. For as long as she could remember, William had always had a glass of wine with dinner, especially after her mother had left them. Once Mallory had turned twenty-one, she had also picked up the habit of relaxing with a glass or two in the evenings.

"Busy! Pleased to be home." He smiled, hanging his car keys up and putting his briefcase down.

"It's been a long day," he groaned. William was the head of a security installation company, and all of their biggest customers preferred to work with William himself.

"Have you finished for the day?" She nodded toward his briefcase.

"Yes. Thank God!"

"Well then, here you go." Mallory passed him the wine glass, which he took gratefully

"See, this is why you are my favorite child."

"That's lucky, seeing as I'm the only one you have." "The only one I need." William beamed, taking a mouthful of the fruity goodness.

"Ah, perfect. What time's dinner? Do I have time to wash up?"

"Yeah, you have plenty of time. It won't be long until its cooked, but I can leave it to simmer for a while. It tastes better that way, anyway. Helps to bring out the flavors," Mallory smiled, taking a sip from her own glass. "So, whenever you're ready."

"Great," he said, walking towards his bedroom, no doubt to have a shower and wash the day's stresses away.

Mallory turned back to the stove, stirred her chilli meat, before turning the flame down to low, and allowing the pan's contents to simmer.

Turning the radio off, and walking into the living room, she switched on the television, and was greeted with the tune of the six o'clock news; sitting on one of the overstuffed sofas and sipping at her wine, the latest missing woman's photo flashed up on the screen.

"A desperate search is still underway for missing Leilah Wyatt, the twenty-year-old student from Portland, Oregon. She, was last seen at her friend's apartment building the day before they reported her missing. Her friends and family are pleading for help from the public. If anyone has any information relating to Leilah's whereabouts, please call the number on the screen. Her parents will make a formal statement with the local authorities later this evening."

Mallory shook her head sadly at the thought of what the families of the missing girls must be going through. Knowing all too well what it was like for a loved one to be there one day, only to be gone the next. It was such a confusing and heartbreaking time for the ones left behind. Maybe that's why these missing persons cases were hitting her on a personal level. Every day was so damn hard, wondering where their loved ones had gone, and what they had done to deserve their leaving.

Hopefully, young Leilah was just partying hard with her friends somewhere, while being completely oblivious to the frantic search party out looking for her, and not something more sinister.

Picking up her laptop, she typed in the girls' names, searching for any recent articles that had been posted on the four missing women. Clicking on one, she skimmed for any information she had not been aware of, but unfortunately, nothing stood out. Like the three others, Leilah had just disappeared. They had used no bank cards, no surveillance had been picked up apart from their previously known destinations, and their phones all appearing to be switched off. She had just vanished!

"Hey, Mally! I'm almost ready," came a shout from down the hall.

"K," she said, standing up, still holding her laptop, and walking the few steps to the kitchen, searching the article she had clicked on.

Someone must know something! She was pretty positive the police were doing everything they could do. But the sad fact was, some people just did not like speaking to the police, especially in the big cities. They either did not like the authorities and refused to help, or they were just too scared and didn't want to get involved. Maybe private investigators and journalists like herself would have more success at digging. There was only one way to find out, and she was determined to try.

Serving the food onto plates, she carried them both over to the table. Just as William came walking into the kitchen, inhaling deeply.

"This smells great, Mally, thank you." He sat and picked up his fork. "Did you have a good day?" he asked, before shoveling a mouthful of chilli meat and rice in.

"No. Not really. In fact, it's been kind of crappy."

He looked up from his small feast. "Oh, how come?"

"After I went to the store, I realized that I really must have that new color palette, but by the time I had made it to the other store, they were completely sold out!" she said with a mock-horror look.

"Bummer." William grinned, placing another forkful into his mouth. "I know what will cheer you up though."

Mallory looked up from her food, searching his face.

"Thomas called me back…"

"And?" Mallory held her breath

"He said they would love for you to come and stay, just like I knew they would."

"That's brilliant, Dad! Thank you. Did he say when?"

"Well, he said that Susan would make up the guest room straight away… So, I suggested the day after tomorrow? Is that soon enough?"

"That's so amazing, Dad. Thank you."

"You're very welcome, although would you prefer it if I traveled up with you? It would have to wait until the weekend though."

"I'll be fine driving up by myself, Dad. As much as I love road trips with you, I really want to get out there as soon as possible before someone else gets my story."

"Okay, that's what I thought you would say." He suddenly frowned. "You will be okay, won't you, Mally?"

"I'll be fine. That's why you bought me the sat nav, remember? Me and Yoda will get there in no time."

Not long after passing her driving test and buying her first car, William had gifted Mallory the best satellite navigation device he could find. And the first thing she had done was download the Star Wars voices, so she had a choice of characters to lead the way.

"I know you will be fine driving, Mal; you are one of the safest drivers I know," he said, smiling. "I meant once you get there. Remember, you are not far off the ages of these girls."

Reaching across the table for her father's hand. Mallory looked at him with a serious expression.

"I promise you, Daddy, I will always keep my phone and pepper spray with me."

"You'd better. It's going to be really quiet without you here for a few weeks."

"Yep. Whatever will you do?"

"Walk around naked for a start. It's gonna be a cool summer for me!"

"URGH... As long as you put a towel down wherever you sit!"

Both laughing, they finished the rest of their meals, enjoying each other's company.

After clearing the dinner table Mallory emailed Monica, the editor from the Sacramento Times, requesting five minutes of her time. They were on good terms from previous propositions Mallory had contacted her with, and she had accepted a few of Mallory's previous articles which had gone in to print.

Feeling relieved when not long after sending, she received a message back, telling her to come to Monica's office at 7:30am. She will see her before her first appointment of the day.

After she had finished organizing her pitch for tomorrow morning's meeting, she walked back into the small and cozy living room to watch her favorite sitcom with William and finish the rest of the wine bottle. After a while, William stood, yawning.

"I'm off to bed. Night Mal."

"Night Daddy." She smiled, sitting with her phone and writing a shopping list of things she needed to get before leaving for Amity.

She could not wait to go riding and could only imagine what the scenery was like. Amity was near Lake Anwar, and looking online, it looked absolutely breath-taking.

Hearing her phone beep from its text tone, Mallory picked it up to read Teresa's name on the screen. Smiling, she opened up a message from her long-time best friend. It was unusual for them to have a day where they hadn't checked in with each other, either by text messages or phone calls. Unfortunately, it had been a couple of weeks since they had physically seen each other, but they always knew what was going on in each other's lives.

Teresa: You will NEVER guess what happened to me today!

Mallory: What? With your luck, it really could be anything.

Teresa: I went to yoga on my lunch break, we were in the middle of doing the Downward dog pose… And I kid you not… My yoga pants split! Right at the ass seam!

Mallory: NOOOOOOOOO!!!!

She snorted. If it was going to happen to anyone, it would happen to Teresa Santos!

Teresa: My life is ruined!

Mallory: Oh no! Did anyone see anything? How embarrassing!

Teresa: Only half the class! The poor woman bent over behind me almost got one of my ass cheeks in her face! THE SHAME!!

Mallory: Oh Teresa!

Laughing harder, she pictured the scene of Teresa's voluptuous Latina curves, with one of her butt cheeks poking out of her yoga pants and into someone's poor, unexpected face!

Teresa: I know! I am never going back there EVER again!

Mallory: Talking about lunch breaks, do you fancy meeting me tomorrow on yours? I've got news to share.

Teresa: Ooh Sounds interesting!

Mallory: I'll meet you at the coffee shop near your office if you like?

Teresa: Sounds good. See you tomorrow at the normal time.

Standing up and stretching with an enormous yawn, Mallory noticed the time and realized she had better get off to bed. She had an early meeting, and lots of packing to do tomorrow before her trip.

Turning off the lights and making sure all the doors had been locked and security alarm set, Mallory walked into her bathroom, brushed her teeth, removed her make-up, and took her Medusa-gem piercing out, so she didn't pull it out by accident while she slept.

Stepping into her bedroom, she noticed a rectangular box with a pink bow on top sitting on her bed.

Squealing with delight, and convinced she knew what her dad had done. She ran over to the bed, opened the box, and looked inside. Yes! She really was the luckiest girl.

Thank God for William Taylor! A beautiful man, both inside and out who had raised her single-handily since she was ten, and had always been there to hold and comfort her, drying her tears when she was heartbroken and desperate for her mother. He was the one who had read her bedtime stories and listened to her problems. Her daddy, who was never too busy for Mallory, he had always helped with her homework, and as time went on, college applications. She was very lucky to have a dad like him. He had spoiled Mallory, overcompensated for her mother not being around.

She fell asleep with a big smile on her face, thinking about her dad and knowing she was the proud owner of the new Urban Decay color palette… in beautiful Metallics!

CHAPTER THREE

Pressing record on the camera, he turned to inspect his work.

He had positioned his toy bent over the metal support bar, he had fixed it to the floor for these special occasions.

Her wrists and ankles were bound with the new rope, the leg spreaders separating her hips. He was satisfied she couldn't move.

He whistled.

Eager to obey, his dog stood and walked over, sniffing.

"It's your lucky day, boy!"

His dog was always horny.

It was always a fifty-fifty chance which hole he would get. But he never seemed to mind.

Rubbing canine breeder's musk all over her back and on her exposed sex organs, he sat back on his special chair to enjoy the show.

It didn't take long before the dog began to mount, scratching and clawing her hips and back in the process.

"Good boy!" He laughed.

***

"Good morning," the lady behind the front desk smiled. "Good morning, I have an appointment with Monica Curtis, from the Sacramento Times."

The receptionist smiled and told Mallory the level she needed to go to; she had been here a few times already, so knew exactly where she was going, but she gave the lady a big smile and thanked her.

Riding the levels up in the crowded elevator, Mallory waited until the light had rested on six, before excusing herself past the other passengers and getting out, she made her way over to a smaller reception desk.

"Hey Pascal," she smiled at Monica's French secretary.

"Bonjour Mallory!" They had spoken a few times, so they were on friendly terms. Despite a distinct French accent, Pascal spoke faultless English.

"How are you? Are you well?"

"Yes, I'm great thank you. I have an appointment with Monica?"

"Yes, of course! I saw your name when I came in this morning. It was a last-minute meeting, no? Let me tell the boss you have arrived."

After putting the phone down, he smiled at Mallory. "Monica said to go through."

"Thanks, Pascal." She took a deep breath and walked along the corridor to Monica's office and knocked on the door.

"Yes, come in."

As she entered the room, she found herself looking out of an enormous window; it had a spectacular view of the hustle and bustle of the morning's activities in Sacramento.

Behind a dark wooden desk sat Monica, eating a bowl of cereal.

"Morning, Mallory, you must excuse me. You've caught me eating cornflakes! It was the only time I could see you today."

"It's no problem. I know this is last minute. I'm just grateful that you could fit me in," she said, smiling at the short, gray-haired woman. Monica must have been in her early sixties, with a warm smiling face that Mallory imagined could change in an instant.

"Good. Now shoot. You have ten minutes before my first appointment arrives."

She wasted no time. Mallory took her news pitch out of the folder, along with the article she had cut out of yesterday's newspaper, and passed it across to Monica.

"I am traveling to Amity tomorrow, staying with some friends of my father. Their ranch is very close to Portland, where another girl was reported missing yesterday. Making her the fourth woman to go missing there in the last three months."

"Yes, I am familiar with the story," Monica said, placing her empty breakfast bowl on the desk, re-adjusting her glasses, and opening the file Mallory had handed her.

"I was hoping to attend a few press conferences, interview some of the women's family and friends. See if I can find out if the women are possible runaways? If they are, what are their reasons? Drugs? Family disputes? Work pressures? Debt problems? Who were the last people to see them? Or is there something a lot more sinister going on in Oregon? Have they got a serial killer on their hands?" She looked over at Monica, who was yet to show any expression on her face.

"I'm ready to write a really gripping article, Monica. I have been researching this subject for a while now, and I really feel this experience will be invaluable to my story. I am so ready to sink my teeth into this case."

"Okay, okay." Monica said, slowly nodding while reading her pitch. Finally, looking up and staring at Mallory for a moment.

"Okay, Mallory, see what you can dig up. If you find anything that's interesting and newsworthy, send me your pitch. I think it is something that we could get on board with."

Mallory smiled with relief just as Monica's telephone interrupted them.

"That will be my appointment arrival."

She left the office with a big smile on her face; she had her contact. Now she just needed to find the story.

***

With bags in each hand, Mallory walked into the coffee shop, eyeing up the cakes and pastries that were displayed.

"What can I get for you today?"

"Can I get a black Americano and a cappuccino, please?"

"Certainly, any food for yourself today, ma'am?"

"I'm actually meeting a friend for lunch, but she's yet to arrive."

"No problem, we can take your food order when we bring your drinks over."

"Great. We will sit outside."

"Yes, of course, it's going to be another sunny day," smiled the barista, accepting her card.

Walking back outside, she chose a table in the sun and in full view of the people entering the coffee shop. Making herself comfortable, Mallory pulled out the book she was in the middle of and read while she waited.

It wasn't long before she heard the familiar voice of her best friend.

"Sorry Mal, just as I was about to leave the office, I had to take a call."

Looking up from her book, she smiled to see her beautiful Brazilian friend, with her black bouncy curls framing her face, pull out the chair opposite her.

"No problem. I've ordered our drinks already. You just need to decide what you're wanting for lunch."

"Well, after splitting my pants yesterday, it's probably a good idea to order a salad." Teresa grinned at her, making Mallory laugh. Teresa had the perfect curvy figure Latina women boasted. They both knew she didn't need to lose an inch.

At that moment, a young barista came over carrying their drinks, placed them on the table, and wrote their lunch orders.

"How's work?" Mallory asked Teresa, watching her friend stir four sachets of sugar into her cappuccino.

"Busy. The new client they have given me is getting right on my tits! He just keeps asking me the same questions over and over! It's like he's trying to catch me out on my answers. Maybe it's because I'm young and a woman."

"Well, it better not be! And anyway, he will soon find out you are excellent at your job. I know it stinks, but perhaps he is testing you, until he knows for sure you know what you're talking about?"

"Maybe." Teresa had recently begun working for a Marine insurance company, which was mainly a male-driven business. Mallory was confident knowing her friend knew her stuff. Whatever Teresa put her mind to, she became obsessive in her need to know everything involved in that subject. Countless times Mallory had listened with blank expressions to Teresa talking about claims she had dealt with, involving shipwrecks, while pretending to know what her friend was talking about!

"Once you have made your name known in the company, I bet you won't have these problems anymore. I guess it's the joy of climbing the ladder."

"Yeah, I guess."

Their conversation began turning to mutual people they knew, gossiping while eating their grilled sandwiches.

"So, then Mally, what's your news?"

"I'm off to Amity tomorrow for a week or two."

"What? Why?"

"Remember, I told you about the case I had been following, about those women from Portland? Well, another woman was reported missing yesterday, and I was complaining to Dad about Portland being so far away, when he reminded me about an old college friend of his who owns a ranch in Amity, twenty miles from Portland! A couple of calls later, and I'm able to go stay, and try to get enough information to support my research."

"Wow! That's great. Have you spoken to anyone about your article idea yet? Or are you just going to see what you can find out first?"

"Had a meeting with the Sacramento Times editor, first thing this morning, and she said if I can find out anything substantial, it would definitely be something they would be interested in. So, keep your fingers crossed for me!"

"How amazing would it be, if you found out something which could help find one of the women? I'm keeping everything crossed for you. We will soon be able to take over the world Mally!"

Laughing at her crazy friend, they enjoyed the rest of Teresa's lunch break together before Mallory drove home with her purchases. She had some research she wanted to get on with, and a mountain of packing to do before her trip.

***

"The black or the orange ones?" Mallory asked herself, taking turns moving her feet in front of the full-length mirror, trying to decide what shoes she should take. "Both," she answered, smiling at her reflection.

Sitting on her bed to take both the different style shoes off her feet, she heard William walk in, home from work.

"I'm home, Mally!" he called, walking through and poking his head in her doorway.

"Hey, Daddy. Did you have a good day?"

"Yep. But I can't believe it's not Friday yet."

Mallory smiled up at him. It was only Tuesday, and the week had just started.

"Have you made any plans for this weekend yet?"

"Not yet. I might just sleep."

She laughed at him, knowing that would never be the case. Her father always made sure his diary was full. If it wasn't Mallory or work, it was definitely friends that kept him busy. That's the way it had always been since her mother had gone. He would never allow himself to pause and take a break. Too worried that if left in his own mind, the memories of his wife, and thoughts of her leaving them, would physically kill him.

William Taylor always made sure he was on the go, and that's the way he liked it. It was best to ignore and pretend that deep down, he wasn't a broken man.

"I've been so busy today; would you mind if we just ordered pizza tonight?"

"Sure. Would never say no to pizza, want me to order?"

"Please," nodding as William made his way into his own room.

Zipping up the suitcase and carrying it over to the doorway, she picked up another empty case and placed it on the bed. She wanted to pack her car tonight. She was planning on leaving early the next day and didn't want to wake William before he had to start his day.

Folding various styles and colors of tops, as small as she could, she squeezed in as many as the suitcase would allow. Mallory wanted to take a useful selection, not knowing what she would require and for what the occasion needed.

Closing the lid on the second case, she leaned over with one arm, putting some weight on it and after a brief battle with the zip, she closed it and placed the case next to the other one on the floor.

William came walking through, still towel drying his hair from his shower.

"You want me to put these cases in your car, Mal?"

"Please Dad, they are good to go."

She looked at her bookcase and wondered how many novels she should take. Deciding on two, consoling herself with the thought that if she needed any more, Portland was sure to have lots of bookstores. It was only her vanity case to go now, which she would take with her when she had finished putting her makeup on in the morning.

Satisfied she was ready for her trip, she walked into the kitchen to open a bottle of wine. Fancying something pink tonight, she picked out a Moscato, which had a fruity, refreshing taste, and poured two glasses.

She could hear her father talking to the pizza delivery man outside. She sat on the sofa and sighed happily.

William walked in, carrying the pizza boxes. He sat down beside her and handed Mallory hers before switching on the television.

"So, you all ready to go Mally?"

"Yes, I think so."

She opened the box for her usual spicy sausage pizza and took a slice, telling William about some of the interesting facts she had discovered today. One being that Portland had quite a high number of women who were being reported missing each year.

"I guess with Portland being the biggest city in Oregon, it makes sense to have more missing people than in the other smaller cities," said William.

Mallory nodded in agreement. But what made little sense to her was the pattern in which they seemed to disappear. There seemed to be clusters of missing persons' reports, followed by quiet periods, but with no logical explanations why. It didn't appear to have a seasonal link, for example, people leaving their families and former lives because of depression over the festive periods, with the fluctuating cycle taking place at different times. Nor was there an obvious pattern shown regarding people's class, and with a mixture of ethnicities too.

The only clear number which was repeated was the percentage of missing women under the age of thirty. Which didn't point to middle-aged women, not happy with their lives and wanting something more. Or different, like her mother obviously had done?

After they had both finished with their pizza's, Mallory took both of the boxes and threw them outside in the trash can.

"I dropped into the grocery store after my meeting this morning, and stocked up with some of your favorite meals, and some snacks too. Please try to stay reasonably healthy while I'm away."

"Thanks, Mal. You are a good girl. What snacks?" he asked, making her laugh at him.

"How did the meeting go?"

"Really well. If I can find something interesting to write, Monica's on board with the story."

"That's great. I'm sure if there's a story to be found, you will find it," he said, looking at Mallory proudly.

"Hope so."

"Know so."

Mallory gave him a big hug, telling him she needed to get an early night for her long drive in the morning, and promised she would let him know when she had arrived at the ranch.

"Okay Mally, be good. Stay safe."

CHAPTER FOUR

He stepped into his playpen and secured the door from the inside, looking over to where his toy was slumped motionless on his special chair.

She had screamed what remaining little energy she had left, not that anyone could hear her out here. Especially with the ball gag in her mouth.

Her legs, coated in dried blood, were still strapped in the stirrups, but sat at an unusual angle because of her dislocated hips.

She had a big, thick collar attached to her neck, with a heavy chain connecting her to a hook on the ceiling, which was a little overkill, he admitted. There was no chance of her moving very far after last night's playtime.

Opening the drawer where the other keys were kept, he put the padlock key inside, until he was finished.

He wasn't quite done with her yet.

It was his turn to play now. There were other holes that were begging to be explored and wonders still to be found.

"Take the next right in 500 yards, you will. Leaving the interstate, you must," Yoda directed, startling Mallory. She had been driving along the same stretch of highway for the last 460 miles now.

Looking down at her sat nav, she was forty minutes away from her destination of Elm-Green Farm, feeling the flutter of butterflies come alive in her stomach.

She switched her indicator on and slowed down the car. Turning, she noticed a sign for Salem.

"Ha! Well, every day's a school day," she said to the empty car, not realizing there was another Salem that wasn't in Massachusetts, and had nothing to do with the witch trials. Unless, of course, she was driving in the completely wrong direction!

Popping a mint into her mouth, her mind drifted back to the Rileys'. The previous evening, William had gone into his social media account, showing her some recent photos of the Riley family, so she didn't feel like she was going in totally blind and staying with complete strangers.

They seemed to be a happy family, full of smiles for the camera. Thomas, the same age as her father, was clearly a hardworking man and she could tell from the photo he worked outside because of his weather-beaten complexion and sun-bleached hair. He had his arm around a petite, silver-haired woman, who was looking up at him with adoring eyes. This was obviously Susan, who held in her arms a small, long-haired Chihuahua.

Flicking through, William had pointed out their sons. Aiden, she recognized instantly because of his red hair. He had grown into a handsome man, although he only offered a slight smile for the picture. He held the reins to a magnificent, shiny chestnut horse, seemingly so at peace with the animal.

The next image was a graduation picture, showing someone the complete opposite to Aiden. He was shorter and stockier with light brown hair; he looked directly at the camera with an easy-going smile and a sparkle in his baby-blue eyes. They had guessed this was Cole, and she was looking forward to meeting him.

Skipping through photos of the ranch had excited Mallory. It was so big and beautiful, and she could really picture trekking through the mountains on one of their many steeds when she wasn't busy investigating.

Mallory's face flushed. They weren't the only photos that had excited her. The last was a picture of Noah. Standing tall and proud in his Marine Corps 'Dress Blues'. He really had grown into a stunning-looking man. He was tall with a stocky build, and had dark brown hair, which almost looked black, and big golden-brown eyes. Noah was certainly very easy on Mallory's eye, and it disappointed her she wouldn't be meeting him. It was very doubtful he would be home on leave while she was visiting.

"Turn left, you must. Reached the destination, you have," Yoda informed her.

"Here we go." Taking a deep breath, she stopped the car. Opening the door and stepping out, she stretched her legs. That had been a very long drive! She had set off just before 5am and had been traveling for twelve hours, including the stops she had made. She walked over to the wooden gate which had potted flowers on either side, and a rose-wood arch connecting the entryway. A big sign hanging from the top, which read, 'Welcome to Elm-Green Farm', engraved in italics.

Releasing the big cast-iron latch, she opened the gate, returned to her car, and drove in. Closing it after her, she breathed in deeply. The air was so much cleaner out here.

Getting back in her little car, she made her way up the winding driveway; it looked so pretty, with cherry-blossom trees lining either side. Driving further up, the tree line ended, and the ranch house came into view. She whistled under her breath; it was beautiful!

She pulled into an appropriate spot next to two identical silver trucks and switched off the engine. Placing the sat nav and her phone in her bag, she walked up the three steps leading to the red front door, which also had big flowerpots on either side, and pressed the doorbell. After a few moments, the door opened.

"Hello," Cole said, giving her a big smile, flashing his perfectly straight white teeth.

"Hi… Cole, right?"

"Yep, the one and only… I take it you must be Mallory?"

"Yes," she said, smiling and holding her hand out. "Pleased to meet you."

Cole took her hand and pulled her in. "We give hugs round these parts," he said, enveloping her in a bear hug, making Mallory laugh.

"You horrid boy!" a woman's voice shrieked from behind them, laughing too.

Cole released her and looked at his mother. "Just giving her a warm welcome," he smiled cheekily.

"Mallory. Wow, it's lovely to see you. I'm Susan," said the very elegant-looking woman.

"Hello Susan, nice to meet you… again." A yapping little dog came running up to Mallory and started sniffing at her feet.

"This is Hercules… Say hello to Mallory, Hercules." Susan picked up the chihuahua, and Mallory smiled, recognizing the little dog from the photos.

Leading the way into the kitchen, Susan asked her how the drive went.

"It wasn't too bad. I listened to the latest Stephen King book on the way, so it went quickly really."

"Stephen King? I'm more of a Danielle Steel kind of guy," said Cole, grinning at her and making her laugh again.

"Please believe nothing my son says," Susan said sternly. "He much prefers the periods. Catherine Cookson is more his style."

Mallory could see exactly where Cole had gotten his sense of humor from.

"Cole, honey, why don't you collect Mallory's things from the car, so she can go to her room and freshen up."

"Sure, let me just get my butler's outfit on," he cheekily replied.

Mallory searched her bag for her car keys and handed them to Cole gratefully.

"Thank you," she smiled, already feeling comfortable with her new friend.

"No problem," he said, before disappearing towards the entrance.

"Would you like a drink, Mallory? Or something to eat? Dinner won't be long, but I'm sure I can rustle you up something quick if you are hungry?"

"No thank you, I had a sandwich when I stopped for gas a few hours ago."

She looked around the impressively spacious kitchen; it had a comfortable and rustic feel, with a warm and savory smell. An enormous table that sat around eight people, with a long window that made the room feel bright and cheerful.

"A coffee would be great though, please."

"Sure."

Susan sat the little dog down, who ran straight back to Mallory and carried on with his sniffing inspection.

"Hercules, huh?" Mallory bent down to pet the tiny dog.

"Yep. Be careful of your fingers, though. He can be a little tinker! Although he seems to like you. Milk and sugar?"

"Neither, thank you," Mallory smiled, standing and taking the cup graciously. "You have a beautiful home."

"Thank you, you are very sweet. Cole will give you the grand tour once he's gotten your bags."

The front door opened, causing little Hercules to bark and begin his security duties again.

"He seems to be a great guard dog. Bet you don't need a house alarm with Hercules around," Mallory said, and laughed.

"He definitely has little dog syndrome," said Cole, walking back into the kitchen with a suitcase in each hand, Hercules still yipping excitedly around his feet.

"The beast we call him, well... I call him."

"You leave my baby alone!" Susan pretended to scowl at her youngest son.

"He's really my replacement," said Cole, "just not as handsome."

Laughing, Susan gave him a playful slap on the shoulder,

"Stop being cheeky and show Mallory to the guest room." She turned to Mallory. "Dinner will be ready for about 6, so you've got an hour to freshen up and make yourself feel comfortable, don't be afraid to ask for anything and make yourself feel at home."

It really is like the perfect family atmosphere here. She inwardly smiled.

"Follow me, my lady, we'll have to take the stairs. The elevator is out of order."

"Right behind you," she answered, eager to see the rest of the house.

Walking back into the entrance hall, she noticed an old-decommissioned Winchester rifle hanging proudly on the wall, next to family photographs of them riding horses, or of various pictures of the Riley children when they were younger.

Still holding her coffee cup, she followed Cole up a big wooden staircase and past what she could only presume to be bedrooms. He opened the door to one of them and they both walked into a comfortable, wood paneled room with a large solid mahogany framed bed, holding what looked like a very comfortable, ready-made mattress.

"This is you."

"Wow, this is great," Mallory said, walking fully into the well-lit room. There was an enormous window that offered a panoramic view of the grounds. She could see a block of stables that wasn't far from the house, with beautiful green hills covered in grass and trees on the horizon.

The room had a small connected bathroom, complete with a shower that hung over a bath. Perfect after a day's riding.

"I'll leave you to freshen up. My room's third on your left. If you need anything, just holler! You have an hour till grub's up," said Cole, smiling and placing the suitcases down by the bed.

Alone in her new temporary room, she decided she would run herself a bath. The tub looked very welcoming. While the water was running, she sent William a quick text message, knowing he'd be driving home from work, letting him know that she'd arrived safely, and would call him later.

Mallory unpacked her clothes and found new homes for her things. It was so quiet out here, so peaceful, with the occasional sound of a horse's neigh. She guessed the horses were getting led into the stables for the night. She would need to wait until the next morning to see them.

Turning off the bath's faucets and getting undressed, she sank into the bubbles and closed her eyes. Making a mental note to search online for any updates on the next press conference, which was scheduled with the provision that Leilah Wyatt would still be missing.

Dressing for dinner, Mallory decided upon wearing baggy black-and-white checkered trousers, teamed with a tight, gray t-shirt. She brushed her long black hair down and refreshed her make-up. While putting on her orange shoes that showed her neatly black painted toes, there was a knock on her room door.

"Oh, Mallory…" Cole called. Smiling, she opened the door.

Cole gave a long, low whistle when he saw her. "Well, I'm feeling underdressed."

Mallory playfully slapped him on the arm.

"Oh, shut up," stepping out of the room and into the hallway. Cole hooked his arm, Mallory linked hers through, and they both headed down to the kitchen together.

As they were walking down the stairs, she started inquiring about some of the photos that were hanging on the walls, while Cole answered in his best David Attenborough voice, making her laugh.

The conversation taking place in the kitchen abruptly ended as they made their way into the room. Thomas was standing by the counter, quietly talking to Susan, while a big black and gray Australian Cattle dog stood in the middle of the kitchen, watching them enter.

Mallory felt very relieved to be standing next to Cole.

"Mallory, hello! Well, you've certainly gotten taller since I last saw you," Thomas smiled.

Smiling back, she was about to return his greeting, when she heard a low growl coming from behind her, turning her head to see another cattle dog, standing beside a red-haired man, who was looking down at Cole and Mallory's linked arms. He had icy-blue eyes that appeared to be giving Mallory the once over.

"Hello, you must be Aiden."

"Hello," Aiden replied, walking past her and taking his place up at the table. A far cry from Cole's welcoming hug.

"Don't mind the mutts," said Cole, and more quietly to Mallory, "Or my brother! Come on, let's go eat." Leading her to the table, Mallory sat opposite Aiden, not knowing if she would rather sit away from the unfriendly looking dogs or the frostiness of Aiden Riley.

"Sammy, Blue, heel," Thomas commanded them, and both the dogs obediently walked to the head of the table where Thomas sat, sitting down on either side of his feet.

"So, Mallory, how is that old man of yours?"

"He is very well, thank you." Mallory smiled, thinking of her father.

"I've been trying to get him to come up for a visit. Thank you darling," Thomas said, as Susan placed a steaming plate down in front of him.

"But we got the next best thing." He smiled, looking at her.

"He's always so busy with work," Mallory explained, "He has some very demanding clients."

Susan placed a plate of spicy chicken, broccoli and rice in front of her.

"Glass of wine, Mallory?"

"Yes, please Susan. This looks amazing. Thank you."

"I'll get the drinks, Mom," Cole said, standing. Mallory almost pulled him back down next to her! She really didn't feel comfortable without him by her side. Perhaps it was the two cattle dogs gazing at her intently, or maybe it was Aiden who sat very stand-offish, almost looking down his nose at her.

"I hear that you have come for research purposes too, Mallory?" Thomas asked.

Mallory nodded. "I have been researching missing people's reports and the reasons for their disappearances. I've been following the reports about the four missing women from Portland. I'm sure that you are aware of…"

"Not really. We rarely pay much attention to the news," he laughed. "We are in our own little corner of the world up here," said Thomas, putting his hand over Susan's on the table.

"That must sound strange to you, being a journalist. I hear that you have had some articles printed. Your dad is very proud of you. What were they about?" Thomas asked, eating his food.

"Yes, nothing very major yet, but The Sacramento Times has published a few. One of them being about the terrible wildfire we had last year, which devastated a local vineyard, destroying all the season's wine-grape crop."

"That is truly horrific," Cole gasped dramatically, clutching the wine bottle he had just gotten from the wine rack, making everyone at the table laugh, except for Aiden.

"But apart from some friendly protests and fashion articles, I've found it difficult to find a story to get published. Working freelance is a very competitive industry."

"I'm sure that it must be. I also heard of your love for horses, Mallory. Well, we have a few of those." Thomas grinned.

"Oh yes! Unfortunately, it's been a while since I've ridden."

"You must take Mallory riding tomorrow, boys," Thomas said to his sons.

"Actually, I won't be around tomorrow," said Aiden, excusing himself. Mallory was almost too embarrassed to look up in his direction.

"That's okay, Mallory. I know all the great places to show you. Aiden would only slow us down anyway," said Cole, then mock whispered "He rides like an old man."

"Great! I'm very excited to meet the horses," she said, giving Cole a big smile.

At that moment, little Hercules came walking backwards through into the kitchen, dragging behind him what was obviously one of the bigger dogs' bones, and was twice the size of the little dog. Cole looked straight at Mallory.

"See? I told you he was a beast!"

CHAPTER FIVE

"Wakey, wakey," he smiled cheerfully while heating the crocodile clips with the blowtorch.

Picking up the glowing red clips, he walked over and clamped one onto each of her nipples, the smell of burning flesh filling his playpen.

Her eyes jolted open, and a very low guttural noise began to build inside her. Turning back to the workbench, he heated the last clip.

"Now where should we clamp this one?" he asked her, holding the red-hot clip up in front of her.

She began shaking her head furiously as he opened her legs and placed it on the most intimate part of her.

He stood back to admire his work; this toy made the strangest of noises! He was pleased it had all been recorded. He will get a good price for these videos.

Lifting the chain that was connecting all three clips, he smiled and gave an almighty pull.

That was the last thing the woman saw as she passed out with the pain. Never getting the chance to open her eyes again.

***

Walking down to the kitchen the next morning, Mallory was looking forward to her day ahead.

"Good morning, Mallory," said Susan. "What would you like for breakfast?"

"Morning. Toast would be great, please. And coffee… lots and lots of coffee."

"Done." Susan grinned, taking a mug from the cupboard and filled it from the pot.

"Tom has already headed down to the stables, he said to join him whenever you're ready and he will show you around."

"Great, thanks. I just need this coffee to wake me up properly." She gratefully accepted the cup and inhaled the sweet aroma.

"How did you sleep? Was everything okay?"

"Everything was great. My head touched the pillow, and I was gone. It's so quiet out here."

"Probably all of that driving. It takes it out of you. Cole's still in bed! I think he must still be on his student clock. Late to bed and late to rise," Susan laughed, placing a plate of butter and a variety of jams next to her.

Mallory had found out last night that Cole, being four years younger than her, was in his last year at school, attending The Cronenberg College of Veterinary Medicine. He wanted to work on the ranch with his father and brother, looking after the horses.

Susan placed a rack of warm toast in front of her, and Mallory smiled her thank you. Picking up a knife, she began buttering her toast when Aiden walked into the kitchen.

"Good morning," he said to the room, not looking at Mallory.

"Good morning darling, can I get you anything for breakfast?"

"Not for me, Mom. I'm just going to grab a quick coffee. I'm actually meeting someone for breakfast down at Ricks Place' this morning," Aiden said, making Mallory smile. At least he hadn't lied about not being available today.

Grabbing a cup from the cupboard and pouring himself a coffee, he sat down opposite Mallory.

Feeling uncomfortable, Mallory searched for something to say but kept drawing a blank. To her surprise, Aiden was the first to break the silence.

"So, Mallory. How long are you planning on staying for?"

Almost spitting her coffee out, she answered defensively.

"Just a week or two, until I can find out some information about the missing women. I would like to attend one of the press conferences, maybe have a little dig around myself, and try to write an article for our local paper back home."

"Things must be pretty dull where you live, to have to come all this way for something juicy to write," he said with a sneer.

"Not really," she said sharply. Contradicting what she had said to her father a few days ago. "I'm just very interested in this story."

"Ahh, so when is this press conference happening?"

Sitting up straighter in her chair, she looked directly at him. She couldn't believe how rude this man was being and wondering why he had taken such a dislike to her!

"Well, if the most recent girl who has gone missing, Leilah, still hasn't been found, it will be tomorrow evening."

Nodding, Aiden drained his coffee cup and stood up. Walking over to Susan, who was busy cutting some fruit for her own breakfast, he leaned down and kissed her on the cheek.

"Don't worry about dinner for me tonight, Mom. I'll be out all day."

"Okay love." Seeming completely oblivious to how rude her son was, or maybe just used to his attitude, she smiled up at him.

"Enjoy your day off."

"I'll try," Aiden said to his mother and walked out of the kitchen, not bothering to grace Mallory with any more of his attention.

She had lost her appetite. Taking the rest of her toast and putting it in the trash, she told Susan she was going to meet Thomas up at the stables, not wanting Aiden to ruin her day by putting her in a foul mood.

Walking out onto the front porch, she breathed in the country air. Looking out into the distance, she could see a herd of horses running around a paddock together, and Thomas leaning against a fence, casually talking to another man. One of his dogs, Blue, she guessed, was sitting next to his master, watching her walking in their direction. She had a big smile on her face and the closer she got to them, the less forced the smile became.

"Ah-ha," said Thomas, when he spotted Mallory "Here she is."

The man who Thomas was talking to turned around.

"Good morning, Mallory. Meet Bobby. Bob, this is my old college friend's little girl, Mallory."

"Good morning, pleased to meet you, Bobby."

The man, who must have been in his early thirties, tipped his hat down. "Pleasure's all mine, ma'am."

Mallory stood at the gate next to them, looking into the paddock.

"Wow. Look at them! They are beauties."

"They certainly are," Thomas agreed. The three of them stood watching the horses galloping around in big circles, almost seeming to play with each other.

"Tom!" another man shouted from what looked like a mobile office. "You're needed!" Thomas looked at Mallory apologetically.

"Sorry, Mallory, would you mind if Bobby started showing you around?"

"Of course. No problem."

"Good. I'll try to catch you both up." Thomas smiled.

Mallory continued to gaze at the galloping horses for a few more moments before Bobby asked if she was ready to see more. Leading the way to the stables, Bobby gave Mallory a handful of sugar cubes.

"Here, take these. Women love diamonds, horses love sweets."

Eager to make friends with the horses, Mallory took them gratefully and put them in her pocket.

"So, Mallory, where you from?"

"Sacramento."

"Ahh, here for a riding holiday?" he asked, leading her to the first horse enclosure. "This is Suzy." Bobby smiled, scratching behind the black mare's ear.

Mallory held her hand out with a sugar cube, smiling as Suzy nuzzled it out of her hands.

"Actually no. I'm a journalist, I'm here for work." She laughed, handing Suzy another cube. "It's just a bonus that I'm able to stay at a ranch while doing it."

"What are you writing about? Anything exciting?" He introduced her to Lily, who snorted her hello.

"I'm here to research the reason Portland has such a high number of missing persons."

"Ooh, yes! And those poor missing girls too."

They moved along to the next enclosure, where Honey already had her head out, nosily watching them.

"It's scary. I've got two sisters around their ages. You need to be so careful these days, don't you?" he said sadly, while Mallory was busy talking softly to the chestnut mare, giving her a sugar lump.

"Hopefully, they will be home soon," Bobby chatted away, walking with Mallory to another enclosure. "This beauty is Bella."

"Hello Bella," Mallory whispered. Holding out her hand so the horse could smell her, before giving her head a stroke.

"Especially young Harriet," Bobby exclaimed, snatching Mallory's attention.

"Harriet Dolan? Do you know her?"

Bella, the horse, snorted her disapproval. Smelling the sugar cubes, she nudged Mallory with her nose.

"Sure do. She often rides here. It's so sad and feels so close to home when someone you know disappears."

Mallory stared at him, not yet knowing what to say. He had taken her completely by surprise.

"Was she riding here the day that she went missing?"

"No, not that day. She must have gone riding at another ranch, or was going somewhere else and not telling her parents where. The police came here, asking questions, but we never saw her that day, and her name wasn't in our books," explained Bobby, referring to their riding lesson diaries.

Mallory closed her mouth after realizing it had dropped open.

Giving Bella her long-awaited sugar, Bobby carried on. "A group of us even took the horses out around the mountains, to check she hadn't gone on a trek alone and gotten lost. But we found nothing, it's just dreadful."

She nodded in agreement as they walked to meet another beauty.

"Do you have Harriet's home address or phone number? It would be really helpful if I could note them down and speak to her parents."

"I don't see why not. I'm sure her poor parents would welcome anything that could help find her. I know they are crazy with worry," frowned Bobby.

"This is Lexi," he said, rubbing the white horse's head.

Mallory felt stunned and couldn't help but wonder why Thomas hadn't mentioned this last night. He had made it seem like he hadn't known anything to do with the missing women. Unless he really didn't think that seventeen-year-old Harriet Dolan was included in the missing women she was here to investigate.

Frowning, Mallory dug another lump out of her pocket and offered it to the horse. Walking over to the last stall, a beautiful brown bay with jet black hair, was waiting patiently for her turn of attention.

"And this girl is your ride today. Meet Roxy, she is a nice hack. A real beauty."

Offering the last of the sugar cubes, Mallory stroked behind Roxy's ears, gently saying her greeting.

"I'll make sure she's saddled up and ready for you guys." Bobby smiled, "Whenever Cole graces us with his presence."

"That's great. Thank you, Bobby, I can't wait."

Slowly making their way out of the stables. Mallory thanked Bobby for showing her the horses and for Harriet's contact details he had written for her. Walking back to the ranch house, she thought about young Harriet. Maybe it was the case. Like Bobby had suggested, Harriet hadn't planned on going riding that day at all. Maybe she had gone to meet a boy? Someone she had maybe met online, and they had planned to meet for the first time. Perhaps it was a catfish situation? Where someone wasn't being exactly honest about who they were online. Mallory gave herself a mental kick! She should have asked Bobby if any of Harriet's friends rode at the ranch, and if he had any contact numbers for them. If he didn't know of any, she was sure Harriet's parents must know her friends.

She walked back quicker; she had a telephone call to make.

Greeted by yapping barks from Hercules, Mallory walked into the kitchen.

"Hey Susan."

Susan, looking up from shaping donuts, gave her a big smile.

"Hey sweetheart, Can I get you a coffee?"

"No, that's okay, Susan. You have your hands full. I can get it."

"Okay, the pot is fresh. Cups are in that cupboard." She nodded in the cupboard's direction. Mallory, already knowing where the cups were kept, walked over, asking Susan if she would like one too, and poured herself a cup.

"No, thank you Mallory. I had one before starting these donuts. I'll remember to keep one aside for you once they're done. If not, you won't get a look in once my boys have spotted them!" She laughed. "They should be ready for when you and Cole go for a ride, if you wouldn't mind taking them to the stables for me? They won't take long to cook."

"Of course, I just need to make a few calls, and I'll be right down."

"Perfect. Cole is conscious now too, so he should be ready when you are."

Walking out of the kitchen, little Hercules followed her until she got to the foot of the stairs. He looked up at Mallory and back towards the kitchen, seeming to be in two minds to where he would rather be. Mallory began walking up and smiled when Hercules decided he would rather be with his master than to follow Mallory. He's so cute, she thought. Maybe she would get one for herself.

Sitting in her room, she dialed the number that Bobby had written for her. After two rings, a man answered in a sad but hopeful tone.

"Hello, is that Mr. Dolan?" Mallory asked, feeling almost guilty, knowing her voice wasn't the one the man on the line wanted to hear.

"Yes?"

"My name is Mallory Taylor, and I am a reporter writing an article about the missing women. I was wondering if it would be possible to meet for a coffee? Just so I could ask a few questions for the paper I write for? I know you and your wife are going through a really hard time right now, but I'm hoping my article might help in reaching out to Harriet? Or maybe to jog someone's memory of seeing her?"

"How did you get my number?" he asked sharply.

Mallory could sense this wasn't going as well as she had planned.

"I'm actually staying with some friends of my father, the Rileys. Up at Elm-Green Farm? Where Harriet rides. We are all dreadfully concerned about Harriet, and would like to help in any way we can. I write for the Sacramento Times; we are hoping a wider audience would be a good way to help."

There was a lengthy silence, and Mallory was feeling very naïve about making the call. She didn't want to upset anyone. She held her breath, expecting to hear the dial tone of the line being disconnected.

"Okay. I guess it wouldn't hurt. We will not turn away any help. I guess you could come over at the end of the week. That's if Harriet isn't home by then," he added, with hope still in his voice.

"Of course. Hopefully she will be." Mallory frowned.

Unfortunately, it was coming up to a month since Harriet had gone missing. So, it was doubtful she would be, but Mallory hoped she was wrong in her assumption.

"Sunday, then. If she's not back. Ten should be okay. Do you have our address too?"

"Yes, I do. Thank you, I won't take up much of your time, Mr. Dolan."

"Okay," he said, and disconnected the call.

Mallory shook her head sadly and quickly sent Teresa a text, updating her on the discovery of Harriet riding at the ranch, and about the interview she had just arranged with the girl's parents.

She put her phone on charge, not wanting to take it riding with her, in case she smashed the phone's screen. Standing up, she tied her long hair into a ponytail, reapplied her lip gloss, and pulled her riding boots out of the wardrobe before putting them on.

Walking down the stairs, the mouth-watering smell of donuts cooking made her stomach rumble.

"They smell amazing, Susan," Mallory said, walking over to the plate that was piled up with fresh donuts.

"Ah, perfect. I'm pleased you think so. Thank you for taking them to the boys for me. Just make sure you grab one before they all go. Cole's already up at the stables, getting his horse ready."

"Great, and I definitely will," she smiled, and walked out towards the stables. Feeling the sun warming her back, she looked up to the bright blue cloudless sky, and thought what a perfect day for riding it was. Getting closer to the stables, she couldn't see anyone. Wondering where everyone was, she walked into the mobile that was used for an office, just as Bobby was putting the phone down.

"Hey Mallory, do I smell Susan's donuts?"

"You certainly do," she said, sitting on the chair that was on the other side of the desk to Bobby.

Unwrapping the plate, she offered him one, which he took gratefully, and put the rest down on the desk before taking one for herself.

"I forgot to ask you earlier, Bobby. Does Harriet have any friends who ride here at the ranch?" she asked, tearing off a piece of dough and popping it into her mouth, emitting a groan as she did so.

"To tell you the truth, Mallory, I don't think Harriet has many friends, period. Certainly not at the ranch. She's a very shy, quiet girl. I guess that's why she was always wanting to be with the horses," he explained.

Mallory nodded, understanding the type of girl he was describing. Lots of kids with social anxieties often found it a lot easier to make friends with animals instead of their peers. Which was probably the same reason Mallory felt a strong connection with them, too. She had suffered with anxiety ever since her mother had left her.

"It's a shame, though," he said, shoving the rest of the donut into his mouth and eyeing another one. "She is such a sweet girl."

Just then, Thomas and Cole walked into the office.

"Mallory, I'm sorry about earlier."

"Please don't apologize, Thomas. I know you are a busy man at work," she said, and smiled at him.

"Are those mom's donuts?" Cole gasped, grabbing one.

"They certainly are."

Thomas took one too, and within minutes the empty plate held just the evidence of sugar.

"You ready to ride, Mallory?" Cole asked her.

"Roxy's all ready for you, as promised," Bobby smiled.

"Thank you, Bobby. I'm so excited!"

Mallory walked out and over to the mounting block. Cole and Bobby walked towards the water troughs where Roxy and a beautiful white gelding were tied.

"How long has it been, Mallory, since you last rode?" Thomas asked her.

"Not since I started college. Must be around five years ago now."

"You take it easy, then. Although Roxy is a great ride."

Bobby untied Roxy, walked the brown bay mare over to her, and lined Roxy up to the mounting block. Mallory stepped up, put her left foot into the stirrup, gripped the saddle, and pulled herself up and onto the horse.

"Thanks, Bobby," she said, taking the reins.

"Enjoy, Mallory. See you both back at the house," Thomas said, stroking the horse's neck.

Walking Roxy over to where Cole was waiting patiently on his white gelding.

"Well, he's very handsome."

"Mallory, meet Artax. Artax meet Mallory,"

"From 'The Neverending Story'?"

"Of course." He grinned as they both trotted toward the mountains.

*** *** ***

Stepping down from Roxy, and passing the reins back to Bobby, Mallory was all smiles.

"That was amazing! It felt so good to be back on a horse again! And the scenery around here is truly beautiful. Thank you, Roxy." She stroked the horse, giving her a kiss on her muzzle. "You are such a good girl," she cooed.

"I'm pleased you enjoyed your ride. I'll book her out for you anytime," said Bobby.

"Oh yes! I would love to take her out again. Although I might need to give my butt a rest for a couple of days first," she said, laughing and rubbing at her tired muscles.

They walked back to the ranch house, and she thanked Cole for showing her the sights.

"You are so lucky to live here! It really is so beautiful, and being able to ride whenever you like. I'm very jealous," she grinned, nudging him with her shoulder.

"I guess. You take a lot for granted when it's your norm. And I'm too busy partying at college to miss this place."

Walking into the house to Hercules usual greeting, the kitchen was emitting the most wonderful smells. Susan had been busy.

"Oh, I'm excited for dinner!"

"Smells like mom's been slow cooking ribs."

"Hey you two! Did you enjoy your ride?" said Susan, looking up from a half-finished puzzle.

"It was great!"

"Mallory has a sore ass now. She will need to soak. If not, she will walk like she's shit herself soon."

"Cole! Honestly! I swear to you Mallory, I brought my son up… Not dragged him up, like his vocabulary suggests!" Susan said, jabbing a puzzle piece she had in her hand in Cole's direction.

"I hate to admit it, but I think Cole maybe right! Have I got time for a bath?"

"Yes, sweetheart, of course. Dinner is at 6."

Looking up at the big kitchen clock that hung on the wall, she had an hour to search for any updates on the missing women and to have a nice, long bath.

"Great, although Cole may need to carry me up the stairs," she said, smiling and before she knew what was happening, Cole lifted her over his shoulder in a firefighter's carry, while she squealed in surprise, and walked her out of the kitchen and up the stairs with the sound of Susan's laughter trailing from behind.

***

"Would you like red or white wine, Mallory?" asked Thomas, while opening the back door to let both of the cattle dogs in.

"Oh, white would be nice please," she smiled back, sitting at the table.

She watched the dogs come in. They were so unusual-looking, almost hyena-like. One went straight to the water bowl and the other sat down near Thomas's usual place at the dinner table.

Walking back with a bottle of pinot, Thomas opened the bottle when Cole walked into the kitchen.

"Ass feeling better now, Mal?" he asked, sitting next to her.

"Yes, not so numb now," she laughed.

Pouring them all a glass of wine, Thomas sat down.

"I was saying to Cole earlier, it must be lovely living on a such a beautiful ranch, and being able to ride whenever you want to." Mallory smiled. "How long have you had the ranch for?"

"We first bought the land around twenty-five years ago now," he said. "After I left college, I lived with your dad for a while in California. Then I met Susan." Smiling at his wife, who was busy serving food onto plates. "And your dad met your mom."

Mallory squirmed in her seat, which was her normal reaction whenever someone mentioned her mother. Thomas carried on, unaware of her discomfort.

"We rented our first little apartment there. We used to see your parents a lot in those days," Thomas told her, taking a sip from his wine, "It wasn't long after Aiden had arrived, and Noah had just turned five, when we finally had our deposit for this place. It had always been a dream of mine, to own a riding ranch." He smiled. "When we got our first few horses, your parents used to come here for their holidays and teach you how to ride. So today wasn't your first-time riding at the ranch."

Mallory gave a tight smile, picked up her wine glass and took a big sip. Cole, seeming to pick up on her unease, asked Mallory what her plans were for the next day.

"I need to go to tomorrow evening's press conference for missing Leilah Wyatt, but apart from research, I have nothing else planned."

"Well, I was thinking maybe we could take the boat out and go fishing?"

"Lake Anwar?" she asked excitedly.

"Yeah! You are familiar with it?"

"Online, yes, it looks beautiful. And I haven't been fishing in years."

William used to take Mallory on fishing trips during the school holidays, something they had both enjoyed and looked forward to doing.

"Perfect," he smiled, just as Susan carried their plates over, full of mouth-watering BBQ ribs, baked potatoes and buttered corn.

"This looks amazing Susan, thank you."

***

"Seriously Teresa, he is such an asshole! He might as well have asked me how long he would have to put up with me for!"

"What a dick!" Teresa said, referring to Aiden.

"Uh-huh, but Cole is a real sweetie. He took me riding today. It was great getting back on a horse again, it's been years."

"What's your dad's friends like?"

"Susan's lovely. Thomas seems nice, although I think it's so strange when I mentioned the missing girls to him, he never mentioned one of them riding at the ranch. That's weird."

"It is weird. Although these hillbilly types aren't the most intelligent people," said Teresa, making Mallory laugh.

"I wouldn't call them hillbillies, Teresa."

"Well, if all they do is shovel horseshit every day, it's not really exercising the brain, is it?"

Shaking her head at her crazy friend, she told Teresa about her and Cole's fishing trip the next day.

"And then I really need to get my detective hat on! This place makes it too easy to forget I'm here for work and not on vacation."

"When did you say you have the meeting with the missing girl's parents?"

"Not until Sunday. But I have a press conference to attend tomorrow evening. I'm hoping I will be able to find out some of the other missing women's parents or friend's numbers, so I can ask them a few questions too."

"Yeah. Someone must know something," Teresa said, echoing Mallory's thoughts.

After listening to news on Teresa's side of life, they said their goodbyes, with promises to speak again in a few days' time.

Feeling tired out after her eventful day, Mallory took off her makeup and changed into her pajamas. Climbing into the very comfortable bed, she opened her book. She had just gotten to the end of a chapter when she fell asleep with her book still open and the lamp left on.

CHAPTER SIX

Piercing the skin with his scalpel blade, he pushed down harder and dragged down.

If collecting his playthings was the exciting part, then the disembowelment of them was definitely the most fascinating.

Inspecting the organs as he removed them, he squeezed part of her digestive system, watching the sludge of juices oozing out, and wondered what her last meal had been.

Not finding much, he had forgotten to feed her while she was in his care. He sniggered as he threw the intestine into a bucket along with the other organs, to sort through later.

Once she was fully gutted, he began to fill her empty cavity with rocks.

Lots and lots of rocks.

***

While Cole was hitching the trailered boat, Mallory sat in one of the Riley's three identical trucks. Turning the rear-view mirror her way, she reapplied her lip gloss, and put on her sunglasses, before Cole opened his door and sat in the driver's seat.

"You might want to readjust that," she said, smiling cheekily.

"That's okay, I don't use it, anyway."

"I really hope that's a joke." She laughed as Cole winked at her, turning on the ignition.

It was a warm, sunny day, and Lake Anwar was only a few miles away from the ranch. Listening to the rock band, AC/DC, they drove the fifteen minutes in comfortable silence as Mallory gazed thoughtfully out of the window, enjoying the beautiful countryside.

Once they had arrived at the lake, Cole spun the truck round to line the trailer up with the boat ramp.

"Do you need me to get out and direct you back?"

"Pfaff, I got this!"

As he reversed, the trailer started drifting off towards the ramp wall.

"Oh, yeah, you've definitely got this."

"I don't think the ramp is very straight! Let me try this again," he said, sheepishly.

On the second attempt, the trailer went too far the other way.

Trying not to laugh, Mallory asked, "Do you want me to do it? Promise I won't tell anyone you needed a girl to do it for you."

Cole glanced sideways in her direction with a raised eyebrow. "You know if you want to be useful, you could get out and see me back."

Both now laughing, Mallory jumped out and between them they got the boat in the water.

Parking the truck, they unloaded their rods, tackle boxes, and the cool box that Susan had packed for them, with sandwiches, snacks, and cold drinks. They were both in excellent spirits as they walked back to the boat, eager to begin.

Once they were out on the water, Cole steered them to an appropriate, quiet section of the lake, and rigged their rods, Mallory surprising Cole, by hooking her own wiggly bait. After they had both cast out, they sat down comfortably, sipping cans of lemonade.

"So, Cole. Do you have a lady friend back at college?" Mallory asked, interested.

"Nope. That's way too much vagina for me…" he said with a grin.

"Oh wow. I'm sorry. I never realized."

Mallory felt shocked. At no point since meeting Cole did she ever get the impression that he was gay! She was normally quite good at sensing these things. It was the first time that her 'Gaydar' had failed her. Laughing, Cole admitted he had come 'out' to his brothers, but he was still yet to come 'out' to his parents. Asking him why, not thinking that Thomas and Susan seemed the type to take that information badly, Cole just shrugged.

"It's just never been the right time, I guess. And how would I do it? Just come right out with it, like I did with you just then? I don't know… it just doesn't seem right that way. I did like the idea of hiding in my closet, and when they have finally come looking for me, I would shout from the inside 'I have something to tell you both, that I would like to do through interpretive dance,' then burst out, and do a jump split? But if I'm being honest, that just sounds way too painful," Cole said, looking at Mallory with a completely serious expression.

She stared at him for a moment… Then she laughed. She laughed so hard that it took her breath away, and she didn't think that she could ever stop.

"Stop it Mallory! You're going to scare the fish away!" But that only made her laugh harder.

Enjoying the sun, and getting to know each other better, they were eating their ham and cheese sandwiches when Cole's line tugged. Staring intently at his float, it suddenly dipped, and they both jumped up. Grabbing his rod, he gave it a jerk and began winding the line back, gently pulling his rod.

"We've got one!" he shouted, quoting Ghostbusters.

Still reeling his line-up, a brown trout soon came into view. Mallory, squealing with delight, picked up the landing net, ready to help when needed. After Cole had pulled the fish to the surface, Mallory placed the net underneath. Scooping the trout in, she hauled it onto the boat.

While Cole was unhooking the beauty, Mallory took her phone out of her bag, switching into camera mode, and took a photo of Cole grinning whilst posing with his catch.

"What do you reckon? It's at least a nine pounder!" he asked proudly.

"Definitely! If not bigger."

Both feeling satisfied, they put the fish into the keep net and placed it back into the water. Giving each other a high-five, Cole sat back down to hook his rod up again.

"Have you got someone special in your life, Mallory?"

"Well, I'm mentally dating a few fictional characters. But actual people? Who are not from books? No, not since college."

"Ahh, book boyfriends. I have a few of those too," Cole smiled. "They are the best."

"Absolutely. My phone, laptop, and books take the other side of my bed up… There really isn't enough room for anyone else." She grinned.

After catching another trout and two smaller fish, they soon noticed the air cooling.

"Should we head back?" Cole asked.

"Sure, it's getting a little chilly now."

Cole began to reel one of the rods in, but the line stopped with sudden tension.

"We must have a snag, or we've hooked a big one!" Cole cried out as the rod bent. Pulling at the rod harder, the tension suddenly let go

"Shit! I think we lost him."

Cole began reeling the line up faster. As the line left the surface, they were both disappointed to see no fish at the end, but could see there was something else tangled to the hook. Standing closer, Cole reeled it in fully until he could reach it.

"What the hell is this?" he asked, untangling what looked like a nest from his hook. They both looked at each other, seemingly both recognizing what it was at the same time.

"I think it's human hair… blond human hair…." she whispered, feeling the chill of goosebumps rushing through her body.

"It can't be!"

"Look." Pointing to a small chunk of shriveled, white flesh, "Isn't that a piece of scalp?"

"Oh, my god!" Cole dropped the bundle of hair on the boat's floor, stepped away, and lost his lunch overboard.

Mallory got one of the plastic sandwich bags from the cooler and dropped the hair in.

"What should we do?" Cole asked, "Should we call the police? Or take it to the station?"

"I think we should call them; in case we need to stay in the same spot."

"Yeah," Cole replied, pulling out his mobile phone, still looking slightly green. "You're probably right."

Once Cole had ended the call with the police, he took all the fishing weights from the tackle box and tied them to the end of a piece of fishing line, dropping it over the side of the boat until it hit the bottom. He tied the other end around the neck of an empty water bottle and placed that in the water too, in the hope this would help the police be able to find the correct area of the vast lake.

Making their way back to land and putting the boat back on the trailer, they both sat in Cole's truck to wait for a nearby officer to come and assess the situation. Both feeling numb with shock about what they had found.

"What are the odds, though? Do you think it's from one of the missing girls? Oh, my god! Leilah has long blond hair," exclaimed Mallory. Thinking about the pictures she had seen of Leilah. "Do you think she went swimming and got tired? Didn't realize how deep it was and got into trouble?"

"I really don't know Mal."

They didn't need to wait long before a police vehicle pulled up beside them and two uniformed men got out of the car. Cole instantly recognized one of the officers.

"Ah! It's Eli, he's one of Noah's friends from school," Cole said, before leaving the truck.

"Hey Cole, I didn't realize it was you who called." Elijah smiled. He was a handsome, African-American, with clean cut hair and a neatly trimmed beard. "I hear you have reported catching something unusual today?"

"Yeah, see what you think," Cole said, as Mallory handed Elijah the sandwich bag with the catch of hair in.

Holding the bag up to the light, it wasn't long before Elijah's expression matched their own, when realizing it was in fact hair that had been yanked off something, with the inch thick piece of scalp at the end. With the length and color of the sample, they could tell it was from a human head.

He passed the bag to his partner, and after a few moments, they gave each other a long, knowing look, before the other man walked away to report back to the station on his radio.

"Where exactly did you fish it from?" Elijah asked, pulling his notepad and pen out of his top pocket.

"We headed about a quarter of a mile, north-west from the ramp. I floated a bottle with some weights on where we were, so hopefully that helps you guys find the right spot."

Nodding, Elijah wrote it down, then placed his notes back into his pocket.

"That was a great idea. It should save us a lot of time." he smiled. "How's the family? Heard from your brother recently?" Elijah and Noah used to play football for the same team back in high school, and they had always met for a beer whenever Noah was home on leave.

"Not for a little while. Which is normally a sign he will come home soon."

"Okay. Well, we will get a search team out here. So, I can drop by the ranch if we need any more information from you guys."

"I'm very interested to see if you find anything. If I promised to keep out of the way, would it be okay if I came back?" Mallory asked, speaking for the first time.

"I don't see why not, as long as you keep your distance and don't affect the investigations."

Driving back to the ranch, Mallory was still feeling stunned and was struggling to believe this was happening. She had been so desperate for a story, and now they had literally just pulled one out of the water! Mallory really hoped she was wrong in thinking it was Leilah's hair, but the coincidence just seemed too high.

"I need to e-mail Monica at the 'Sacramento Times'," she said. "And then I need to get my ass back out there."

Cole nodded. "Wouldn't you rather wait until they find something? This might be a false alarm."

"Do you really think that's going to be the case?"

"Actually no, I don't," said Cole, grimly.

***

As soon as they got back, Mallory went straight up to her room, sat down on the bed, and opened her laptop. She sat still for a moment to gather her thoughts.

Still not really believing what had happened, she typed her article pitch for the Sacramento Times, knowing Monica wouldn't be able to resist her story if the sample came back to be actual hair, or if they found somebody in the lake!

Pressing send on the email, she looked up at the ceiling and took a deep breath. She needed to get back out there!

Quickly changing into her warmer black jeans, she silently thanked herself for packing her soft and warm yellow jumper. Tying up her boots, Mallory grabbed her black jacket that was hanging on the door hook and went back down the stairs. Looking into the kitchen, expecting to see Susan, but instead was greeted by an empty room.

"Susan? Hercules?" she called, knowing if the little dog came running, then Susan wouldn't be far behind. But there was no answer.

Letting herself out of the ranch house and getting into her little car, she drove the short distance back to Lake Anwar, which was easy to find. The plan being Mallory would head up, and Cole would meet her back there later, with some more food and a flask of coffee.

She arrived back at the lake to a very heavy police presence, there were divers already at the scene preparing their equipment. They had cordoned the boat ramp off, preventing Mallory, or anyone else, from getting closer, and they had set portable flood lights up all around the site.

Recognizing Elijah in the distance, she got out of the car and walked toward him, as far as the tape would allow. Once she had caught his eye, she waved and gave him a friendly smile, hoping she could win him over for a potential update.

After he had finished talking to a colleague, he made his way over to Mallory.

"You're back soon. The divers are about to head out and start their search. Hopefully, it shouldn't be too long now."

"Okay, thank you. Just wanted to let you know I will wait in my car; on the off chance you could give me any updates."

"Wouldn't you rather go home to the warm and wait to see if we find anything? This could take a while."

Smiling, she insisted she would rather be here waiting for as long as the search took, knowing there was little he could do as long as she was standing outside the cordon.

The sound of a boat engine interrupted them. Looking over, they could see the divers were leaving the ramp and heading out into the lake.

Nodding to Mallory, Elijah turned and made his way back to the edge of the lake.

She rubbed her hands together; it was getting quite cold now. She could just imagine what the water would be like! She walked back to her car and got in. Making herself comfortable, she sat and watched the search begin.

CHAPTER SEVEN

Checking his phone, he clicked on internet banking. Smiling to himself at the balance.

He was certain there would be some very satisfied customers.

It was a shame his playtime was cut short with her. He still hadn't been able to try his new penetration machine he had made.

The orders had been very dark this time. It wasn't often that somebody wanted doggy-fucking.

But the money was good. Very good.

Maybe the next toy would be just for their pleasure alone.

***

"What?" William shouted. "Jesus, Mal, you've only been there a few days! That's a pretty eventful fishing trip! How sure were you it was human hair?"

"I know. Unbelievable, right? Well, we were fairly sure ourselves, but the fact they've sent the divers down there tells me the police are pretty sure too."

"Yeah, that's not a good sign, is it? What's your next move now?"

"Now it's just a waiting game. I'm going to hang around to see if they bring anything back with them."

"Well, I guess there isn't much else you can do at the moment. How are you getting on at the Rileys?"

"Everyone seems lovely. Well, everyone except Aiden."

"Oh? What's wrong with Aiden?"

"He's just so damn rude, Dad! It's like he's taken an instant dislike to me."

"Maybe he's just shy."

"I don't know. I really don't think it's that."

"Well, hopefully he will warm to you soon."

"Yeah… hopefully…" she said, distracted, looking out of the window to see Cole pulling up next to her.

"I've got to go Dad, Cole's just arrived."

"Okay Mally, keep me updated. Stay safe."

Ending the call, she put her phone back in her bag and unlocked the door so Cole could get in.

"I have come with treats," Cole said, getting in the car with a big bag of food.

"You are amaze-balls."

"Yes, I am." Smiling, he handed her a burger and a big take-away cup of coffee.

"Any updates?"

"No, not yet. The divers went out about two hours ago. Hopefully, we will hear something soon. I spoke to Eli when I got back, to let him know I was going to be hanging around."

"Okay, I'll go out and see if I can grab his attention. Try to find out if they have heard anything yet, while you finish your dinner. I ate mine on the way here."

"Really? I'm too anxious to eat."

"Do it. I ordered you extra cheese." He grinned before leaving her car.

Mallory took a bite of the burger and washed it down with some coffee. She watched Cole as he walked up to the tape, patiently standing there, waiting for Elijah to notice him. Elijah nodded in his direction and walked over. Forcing another bite, she watched the men talking until she couldn't take the suspense anymore. Shoving the rest of the burger back in the bag, she grabbed her coffee and got out of the car.

Walking over to the men, she caught Elijah's last words, "… the M.E will arrive shortly to meet them when they get back to land."

They must have found something, she thought. The Medical Examiner would only attend the scene if the divers have found someone.

"This needs to be kept quiet until we can confirm the details," Elijah said, looking directly at Mallory sternly. "I am only telling you this because I've known the Rileys since I was a young lad, and you were the ones to alert us to the situation. But they are in the process of recovering a body now."

Breathing in sharply. Mallory's eyes widened. They had been right!

"The County Sheriff will probably have a press conference here in the morning."

"Okay, thanks for letting us know, Eli," Cole said.

"No problem. But remember. Keep it to yourselves until then." Tipping his police hat down, he walked back to his standing spot.

Mallory and Cole walked back to her car in complete silence, both lost in their own thoughts.

"Shit. I can't believe it. What do you want to do now, Mal? Should we head back home?"

"Can we just wait a little longer? At least until they get back to shore?"

Sitting in the car, they watched a group of forensics covered from head to toe in white suits and wearing blue masks, leave a big tent that had been erected.

"I don't think it's going to be too long to wait now," said Mallory, just as a boat's spotlights came into view. The boat pulled up to the ramp just as the forensic team walked over to meet them with a stretcher. Carrying the black body bag over, they transferred it onto the stretcher so the crew could take it back into the tent and search the body for any potential evidence before being signed over to the M.E department for an autopsy.

Somberly watching the crew walking back with the body, she couldn't help but wonder who was in the bag. Was it Leilah who her suspicions had jumped to? Or somebody else? Somebody else who was loved and missed, someone who has a family, who will be completely heartbroken to find out the news that their loved one had been found. Dead in a lake.

Once they had entered the tent, Cole and Mallory decided that their best course of action now would be to head back to the ranch and try to get some sleep. Be back at the scene nice and early tomorrow, ready for the press conference.

Cole was just about to leave Mallory's car and get back into his truck when they heard the search boat restart. At first, neither of them thought too much of it, expecting them to remove it from the water. But to their surprise, the boat headed back off into the lake.

Giving each other a confused look, Cole exclaimed, "What the…?" before getting out and walking over to the cordon tape again.

Mallory got out too and stood next to Cole, hoping Elijah would come over and speak to them again.

"Do you think this is just protocol?" she asked him.

"I really do not know."

Noticing them again, Elijah walked quickly over to them, almost seeming as shocked as they were.

"Eli? Is that normal for them to be going out there again?"

"No, it isn't," Elijah answered grimly. "The body they recovered has completely different colored hair to what you guys pulled out of the lake."

"WHAT?" Cole almost shouted.

"They have found more than one body."

***

Following Cole's truck back to the ranch, Mallory's thoughts were running wild! Had they really found the missing women? Is there a serial killer hunting in Portland and disposing of the poor women's bodies in Lake Anwar? Shaking her head, she really couldn't believe the chances of this happening! She'd come almost 500 miles from Sacramento to find some information on the missing women, only to find them while fishing in a lake, not long after arriving! You just couldn't make this story up. Fate is a funny thing, she thought, as she followed Cole through the rose-wood archway.

Stopping, she got out to close the farm gate behind her. Apart from the moonlight showing her the way, she was in complete darkness. Cole had carried on driving the short distance up to the house.

For the first time since being a little girl, Mallory felt afraid.

What monster could have done this? She wondered sadly, hurrying back into her car, every shadow looking a lot more sinister than usual. Shaking the thoughts away, she told herself sternly that she could be completely wrong. It might not be the missing girls after all, and there isn't a serial killer on the loose close by.

Parking her car in front of the house, she could see Cole had left the front door open for her. Walking in, she followed the light that was on in the kitchen.

"Coffee Mallory? Something stronger?"

She just looked at him.

"Something stronger it is then."

Getting two whisky glasses out of the cupboard and placing them down on the breakfast bar, he disappeared in the direction of the living room, obviously in search of the drinks' cabinet.

Mallory looked up at the clock that was hanging on the wall. It was half-past one in the morning, and no doubt Thomas and Susan were sleeping in their bed. Mallory walked over to the breakfast bar that was opposite the long kitchen window and sat on one of the stools. Turning her head, she looked towards the sink, trying to figure out what it was on the plate and defrosting on the drainer. Scrunching her nose up, she realized it was liver. Perhaps Susan was cooking liver and onions for tea tomorrow. She really hoped not. That was one of only a few meals that Mallory hated!

"Why have you got your face all in a twist?" Cole asked, grinning and carrying a bottle of Jack Daniels.

"I'm hoping your mom isn't planning on cooking liver tomorrow," she said, worrying.

"What? No way! She wouldn't be so mean!"

Feeling relieved, she held her glass out for the Jack.

"Why would you think that?" He laughed, filling her glass up with the JD and a little cola.

"I just thought it was liver defrosting on the sink."

Cole looked over to see what she was talking about.

"Oh, I see! No-no, that's the dogs' breakfast."

"Ugh… Haven't your parents heard of kibble?"

"Er no! Only the best for their hairy babies. Dad has been making his dogs' food ever since they were puppies. And I quote, 'They're carnivores, so I will feed them an appropriate species diet. Raw. You don't see wolves getting their meals cooked for them, do you? Or opening boxes of death nuggets'," he said, in his best Thomas voice.

Mallory laughed, sipping at her drink.

"That's what he calls dog biscuits, you know, death nuggets!"

"Well, I'm just relieved that isn't our dinner for tomorrow. The smell of it cooking literally turns my stomach."

"I would have put myself up for an adoption when I was younger, if my mom had made me eat liver and onions."

Finishing their whiskeys, they were soon following each other up the stairs to bed.

"What time do you want to head back tomorrow, Mal?"

"Nine at the latest. Please don't feel you have to come with me, though. I know where I'm going."

"What, and miss out on all the fun?" he said sarcastically, standing outside her door. "Of course I'll be coming with you. Hopefully, we will get some answers to what the hell is going on here."

"I hope so too. I also hope I can get to sleep tonight after this crazy-ass day."

"Well, that's where our good friend Jack comes in to help us. Night Mal. Sweet dreams," he said, walking further up the hall. "For us both," he added, glancing back.

CHAPTER EIGHT

Shit. He couldn't believe it.

His latest dumping ground had been discovered.

After all this time, some of his broken playthings will be found.

He thought the lake had been a good idea…

Looking at the map which hung on the wall, he smiled when he took in all the black pins he had placed to remember them.

He had enjoyed every single one and had made a lot of money out of his playtimes.

He would need to revisit one of his older sites until he could think of a better way to dispose of his used and forever broken toys.

***

Arriving back the following morning, the area was now a different scene from that of the night before. There were various news crews, photographers and journalists present. A platform had been set up away from the cordoned area, facing a different section of the lake. It wasn't long before the County Sheriff stood up in front of the waiting press to read his prepared speech.

"Good morning. Thank you for joining us. Yesterday, at six pm local time, we arrived here at Lake Anwar, following a report of what we suspected to be human hair, found in these waters. We utilized a crew of divers to assist us in our search of the lake." He paused, looking over at the eager faces. The sound of camera shutter clicks, erupting all around them.

"We regret to confirm we have recovered three bodies from the water. We have transferred the recovered bodies to the Medical Examiner's office for formal identifications. Our investigations are underway into the circumstances of these deaths, with no scenarios being ruled out." Pausing again, the Sheriff looked directly into local news station's camera.

"We urge anyone with information to contact the police. Reports can be taken anonymously." Looking back to the press, who were all frantically taking notes, he added, "Thank you for your time. We will hold another conference on Monday morning, when we hope to have more information to give."

"Sheriff! Sheriff," a man from behind her shouted, "Have the bodies been identified as men or women?"

"We do not have that information to give. We are hoping to know more at Monday's conference." Stepping down quickly from the platform, before anyone else could ask questions, the Sheriff and a uniformed police officer walked back towards the cordoned area.

"Wow! Three!" Cole said in a loud whisper as they headed back to the truck. "It's sounding more and more like the missing women, isn't it?"

"Which would mean we have a serial killer on the loose."

They looked grimly at each other before climbing in.

"Fuck! I really was not expecting that," Cole said, shaking his head. "It's crazy! To think we were just floating above them." He shivered, turning the ignition.

"What's the plan now then, Batman?"

"Well, I got the green light from the Sacramento Times for my article, so I need to go back to the ranch and write up the press conference before I submit it. Then I really need to get organized for tomorrow's meeting with Mr. Dolan. They must be out of their minds with worry now that they have found these bodies! Hopefully, they will be identified soon, so it can put them at ease."

Cole looked at her, confused. "Who's Mr. Dolan?" he asked as he drove out of Lake Anwar.

"Harriet's dad."

"And who's Harriet?" he asked her with a frown.

"Harriet Dolan? The youngest of the missing women. She rides at your ranch."

"What?"

"She had told her parents she was going riding the day she never came home, but after speaking to Bobby, he told me she never turned up at the ranch, and she wasn't booked in for lessons either. I really want to find out if there was another ranch that she rode at, or if she had any friends that I could speak to. I'm sure the police must have gone through this already, but it wouldn't hurt if I could ask if they had looked into her internet activity. Double check, she hadn't been talking to any new boys online. Maybe her friends would be more inclined to talk to me, rather than Harriet's parents or to the police? Who knows, but I still want to try. I know after yesterday my attention has changed direction, and I really, really hope Harriet has nothing to do with who was found in the lake. But the sad fact is, Harriet is still missing."

"Of course," Cole said, subdued. "I wasn't aware that any of the missing girls rode at the ranch. But then I have never given any lessons. Aiden did though. I'm surprised he said nothing. Or dad. The police must have spoken to them both about it. I must have still been at school when she disappeared. How long has she been missing for?"

"It will be a month this Sunday. When I speak to her dad, actually."

"Well, that makes a little more sense," he said, nodding. He would have still been away at college when Harriet had first disappeared.

Mallory picked her phone out of her bag and sent Teresa a text update.

Mallory: Three bodies Teresa! Three.

Teresa: Shut the fuck up!

Mallory: Truth! I can't believe it...

Teresa: It's completely insane! I'm still in shock you found them!

Mallory: You and me both!

Teresa: Well, I said I would keep my fingers crossed for you helping to find them, didn't expect for you to fish them out!! I am clearly magical…

Mallory: The bodies haven't been identified yet though, but it's looking very suspicious.

Teresa: VERY SUSPISH! I'm now gonna *cross my fingers to win the lottery!*

Mallory: Maybe you should cross them for the police to find the serial killer they have here on the loose, if they are the missing girls.

Teresa: Shit. Yeah!

Mallory: But you can wish for the lottery win after!

Arriving back at the ranch, Mallory was surprised when Cole opened the front door for her, then turned away.

"I'm going to head up to the stables Mal, I'll see you at dinner."

Walking into the house, the kitchen was quiet, but she could hear a television on. Following the noise, she walked through into the enormous living room, where worn and much-loved sofas filled the room, with Susan comfortably sat on one of them. The room had a high ceiling, with exposed wooden beams, and an open fireplace built into the stone wall at the far end of the room. On the polished, wooden floor was a big, soft shaggy rug, which gave the room a cozy feeling despite its size.

Hercules jumped off of Susan's lap, and went running over to greet Mallory, just as Susan switched off the television with the remote control.

"Wow! I've just seen the news. I really can't believe it was you and Cole who caught the hair when you went fishing! What are the chances? That lake is huge!" Susan said with an amazed look on her face. Standing up, she walked towards Mallory, who was giving Hercules a cuddle by the doorway.

"I know it's crazy, right?" said Mallory, standing up.

"Cole not with you?"

"No, he's gone to the stables."

"Ah, are you feeling hungry? Would you like a sandwich or something?"

"No thanks, I need to write an article, and I really need to get on with it if it's going to be ready for printing this evening. I'm running out of time." Grabbing a coffee instead, Mallory walked up into her room, texting William with her other hand, telling him to buy this evening's Sacramento Times, because her article should be printed in there. Closing the door after her, she sat on her bed, opened her laptop, and typed.

***

Waking up with a start, Mallory laid there, trying to figure out what had woken her. Picking up her phone, she looked to see what the time was. 2:40am. Groaning, she turned over and closed her eyes. But another big thud had them flying open again. What the hell was that? It was normally so quiet in the house. The senior Rileys were always early to bed, and early to rise, normally with the three dogs in the bedroom with them.

Surely the dogs would have reacted if there was someone breaking in… Wouldn't they?

It was most likely Aiden, she thought, straining to hear, but the house had gone deadly silent again. Then a crash. Oh shit. She got out of bed, wearing her tiger-print pink pajamas, and walked over to the bedroom door. Opening it, she poked her head out, held her breath, and listened.

Someone was definitely downstairs! Quickly walking over to Cole's room, she softly knocked on his door. Nothing. Knocking again, harder this time, she put her ear against the door. She could hear Cole snoring loudly. Frowning, she wondered what she should do. She didn't want to wake anyone up if it was just Aiden coming home! But she also knew she wouldn't be able to just get back in bed and go to sleep without knowing for sure.

"Damn it, Cole! If I get murdered, it's going to be all your fault," whispering to herself as she crept as quietly as she could down the stairs, her heart feeling like it was going to pound right out of her chest.

Another rustling came from the kitchen. Mallory looked around, searching for a weapon and finding nothing. Then she remembered the old Winchester the Rileys had hung up on the wall. Standing up on her tiptoes, she reached her hands up as far as she could and unhooked the rifle. Feeling ridiculous, but strangely more confident, she walked into the kitchen. The fridge door was open, with someone rustling inside.

"Aiden? Is that you?" she said, pointing the gun in the fridge's direction.

"No. It certainly is not," came a strange man's voice.

"Step away from the food," she instructed firmly, trying to sound a lot braver than she was feeling. The fridge door closed, putting them both in the dark.

Shit, shit, shit. She had not thought this through!

"Stay where you are! I've got a gun!" she demanded, taking a few steps backwards and feeling for the light switch, which was hard to do, while holding the big, heavy rifle in one arm. Thankfully, she quickly found it and switched it on. Squinting from the sudden light, she looked over to see the most gorgeous-looking man she had ever laid her eyes on! Looking very confused and standing by the fridge, with his hands up.

His face splitting into a grin when he noticed the weapon she was holding up. "WOAH there…. Although I think you're about eighty years too late to shoot that beast!" He laughed.

Mallory put the gun down, her cheeks flushing with embarrassment when she recognized who it was.

"I'm sorry, I thought you were an intruder."

"Oh, but I might be," he said, crossing his arms over his chest and leaning his hip against the counter.

"I know who you are."

"Do you? And who might you be?"

Mallory's face flushed an even deeper shade of red as she stood the old Winchester up against the wall.

"I'm Mallory. I'm William's daughter. From Sacramento."

Keeping eye contact, he walked right up to her, causing Mallory to suck in a breath as she looked into his intense brown eyes.

"Well hello Mallory, William's daughter, from Sacramento. It's nice to meet you." He grinned again as he bent down to pick the Winchester up.

"As you already seem to know, I'm Noah," he confirmed. "And I'd better put this very expensive rifle back in its rightful place. In case anyone else tries to shoot me with it."

"I'm sorry about that…"

"How about you pour us both a drink while I put this baby back? And then you can explain to me exactly why you were trying to shoot me in my kitchen." He smiled. "The Jack is in the drinks cabinet in the…"

"Living room," she answered.

"Yes… It is," he agreed, with a confused look on his face.

Picking out the whisky bottle from the drinks' cabinet in the living room, she walked back into the kitchen and grabbed some glasses. Sitting up at the breakfast bar, like she had done with Cole the previous night, she poured their drinks.

Noah joined her back in the room and walked over to the breakfast bar, sitting on the stool next to her. She wished he had sat further away. She seemed to have trouble breathing when he was close.

"So, Mallory. Are you here for a riding holiday? Is your dad here too?"

"No, I'm a journalist," she explained, telling him all about her research and the four young women who were missing in Portland, which bought her here, and what had occurred on her and Cole's fishing trip.

"You actually caught one of the missing women's hairs?" he asked, looking astonished while refilling their glasses.

"No identities have been confirmed yet. Hopefully, we will know on Monday though."

"I have missed a lot," he said, looking at her. "I'm here now though."

"How long are you on leave for?"

"Around five weeks, unless we get called back."

Mallory drained the rest of her glass, knowing she should really try to get a couple more hours of sleep, although she was wide awake speaking with Noah.

"I really need to get some sleep before my meeting with the Dolans tomorrow."

"The family of the girl who rides here?" he asked, and Mallory nodded.

"And I really need to get back to making my sandwich." He smiled; his eyes were almost catlike. She could easily get lost in them, she thought as she stood up from the stool.

"Yeah… I'm really sorry about that."

He laughed, a deep husky sound. "Goodnight, Mallory. William's daughter, from Sacramento. Sweet dreams."

CHAPTER NINE

He knew he shouldn't take this one. She was not his toy to play with.

But who was he to follow the rules? It hadn't stopped him in the past.

He will have to meticulously plan this one. She was a risky take…

He would have to be careful. Very careful.

But she would be worth it.

He felt himself go hard.

***

Waking up to the sound of her alarm a few hours later, she laid there, wondering if last night had all been a dream.

Getting up, she got into the shower and tried to wash the sleepiness away. Dressing smartly for her meeting, with a black pencil skirt and a dark red shirt. She expertly applied her makeup and matched her lip gloss to the color of the shirt she was wearing. Putting on her black heels and leaving the room, she walked down the stairs to the sound of men's boisterous laughter. Mallory walked into the kitchen to see Noah holding Cole in a headlock, with Aiden looking on, laughing. Aiden laughing! It was the first time she had seen him smile, let alone laugh!

"Good morning, Mallory," said Susan, smiling. "We hear you've already met Noah."

After being released, Cole dived behind the table with a shout of "Don't shoot! Everybody down!"

Mallory could feel her cheeks burning again. She had never blushed as much as she had in the last few hours. She really needed her morning coffee!

"Ha-ha," Walking over to get a cup and pouring herself a coffee. Sitting up at the table, she looked down at Cole, still crouching.

"Well, I tried to wake you up, but the sounds coming from your room last night sounded like you were sharing your bed with some kind of farm animal!"

"That hurts," said Cole, standing with his hand over his heart, taking the seat next to Mallory.

Susan had spread the table with bagels, toast, and jams. Cereal, yoghurts, and fresh cut fruit.

"So then, big brother, fancy doing some proper work today?" Aiden asked Noah, still grinning.

Mallory couldn't believe the difference in Aiden! Obviously, the men were very close.

"Of course. I've missed my beast," Noah said, referring to his horse.

"Great," Aiden said. "I actually have a lunch date today, so if you wouldn't mind taking over a few of my jobs?" Looking over at Cole, "I'm always asking Cole to give me a hand, but he's never normally awake much before lunchtime."

"And who are you meeting for lunch?" Noah asked, raising an eyebrow.

"A gentleman doesn't share."

"Aiden's seeing a girl. And he's being very secretive about who it is," said Cole, shooting back after the sleeping comment. Earning a bagel getting thrown at his head from Aiden.

"All in good time, dear brothers," Aiden said, "I'll see you up there when you're ready." Standing up, he left the kitchen to head up to the stables.

Mallory drained the rest of her cup and stood to put her things in the dishwasher.

"You leaving too, Mal?" Cole asked her.

"Yeah, my meeting is an hour away," she said, looking at the clock.

"I'll make us something nice for dinner. A welcome home meal for Noah," said Susan, smiling.

"Don't make a fuss," said Noah firmly, his tone turning icy-cold, creating an uncomfortable silence.

"I love it when you come home," Cole said to Noah, interrupting the moment "Mom makes all the nice food."

Earning him another bagel flying in his direction, this time thrown from Susan.

"You cheeky git!" Susan laughed.

"I'm going before I get concussion," Cole said, getting up from the table and walking out of the kitchen quickly.

Laughing at Cole, Mallory began piling up some of the now empty plates from the table.

"Leave that sweetheart. I'll clear this all up once you have gone."

"Thanks Susan," she smiled. "I should only be gone a few hours."

Walking over to the front door, she gave her bag a last search, making sure she had everything she needed, including the Dolan's address.

"Do you know where you are going?" said Noah as he opened the front door for her.

"I don't have a clue." She smiled, looking directly into his eyes for the first time today. "But I'm pretty sure Darth does."

"What now? Who?"

"Darth Vader!" she said, waving her sat nav.

"Yep, I was right last night. You really are a crazy person," he said, smiling down at her, making her feel slightly giddy. "But, hey I'm sorry for back there. Susan came down not long after you had gone back to bed. I told her what happened. Should have known it would get around the family by breakfast."

"That's okay. I'm used to people thinking I'm crazy." Laughing, she got in her car and turned on the ignition. Noticing he was still standing by the doorway; she gave him a little wave before driving off. Realizing she was still smiling when she got out of her car to open the ranch's gate.

***

Pulling up outside an impressively big gray bungalow, Mallory double checked the address Bobby had written matched to where she had stopped, and turned off the ignition. Looking at her reflection in the rear-view mirror, she took a deep breath and slowly released it. Telling herself she could do this, she stepped out of her car, locked it, and walked up the path.

Knocking on the pale blue door, a tall, thin man with short brown, graying hair opened the door.

"Hello, Mr. Dolan?"

"Yes?" he asked, looking confused. He had obviously forgotten all about their meeting, but after yesterday's news of the recovered bodies, it wasn't surprising their meeting had slipped his mind. Smiling gently at him, Mallory introduced herself.

"Of course, Mallory! I'm sorry, please come in," he said, stepping aside. "I'm afraid we had completely forgotten." Leading her into the living room,

"If you wait here, I'll fetch my wife. She's just out back," he told her, leaving her to sit on the sofa.

Looking around the comfortable room, with light blue walls and cherry-wood flooring, it had modern décor with lots of photos of Harriet, either riding horses, or with her father and a woman who she guessed to be her mom. They all looked so happy, and it seemed there were only the three of them, with no other children featured in any of the photos.

They didn't keep her waiting long, Mr. Dolan walked in with the woman from the photos. She had short brown curly hair, pinned up at the side, with big brown bloodshot eyes that looked like they had been full of tears only moments before. Mallory's heart ached for them.

Speaking softly, Mallory introduced herself.

"Please call me Paul," Harriet's father told her. "This is my wife, Jackie. Can I get you a coffee or water?"

"Water would be great, thank you."

Smiling sadly, Paul Dolan walked into the kitchen to fetch her drink.

"I'm really sorry you and your family are experiencing this," Mallory began as Paul walked back into the room and placed her glass of water on the table.

"Thank you for seeing me. Hopefully, it will help to bring Harriet home. I just have a few questions. I'm sorry if you have been asked these before. Would it be okay if I recorded our conversation?" she said, holding up her Dictaphone.

Jackie nodded, and Paul sat beside his wife, reaching for her hand.

Mallory pressed the record button and placed the recording device on the table next to her glass.

"I understand Harriet said she was going horse riding the day she went missing? Did Harriet ride anywhere else, apart from at Elm-Green Farm?"

Jackie answered, shaking her head "No, she loves it there. Some of her favorite horses are at the Rileys' ranch."

"Does Harriet have any close friends who I could speak to?"

Jackie shook her head again slowly.

"Harriet is a bit of a loner. She has Asperger's syndrome," Paul said. "Her major difficulties are social situations, so she doesn't really have many friends. Certainly, none she would confide in. Which was why we were always happy for her to travel to Amity every weekend. The horses at the ranch are her friends." He smiled.

"How does Harriet normally get to the ranch? Does she drive or get the bus?"

"She does both. She sometimes borrows our car, but we were using it," Paul said regretfully, shaking his head, "and none of the buses that traveled to Amity that day, had any security footage of her getting on."

"How far away is the bus stop she would normally use?"

"Only a ten-minute walk away. There were no sightings of her, or other footage captured. It's like she just vanished."

"Did Harriet use the internet at all? Was there a possibility that she could have been speaking to someone online?"

"The police asked us this. They checked out her computer and tablet just in case she had been speaking to someone she shouldn't have been. But apart from school work and the odd game she played, she had nothing else on there. Harriet isn't into social media, like Instagram or Facebook. She doesn't really understand the point to them." Paul smiled.

"Where does she attend school?"

"Glosserman High. The police have already questioned the students in Harriet's classes. Nothing came of it."

"I hate to ask this, but can you think of any reason Harriet could have run away?"

Mallory felt dreadful and apologized when Jackie whimpered.

"That's okay. I can't help it when people ask us this. Only because I wish there was a reason for her to have run away! But there was nothing," said Jackie, wiping under her eyes. "We are a pretty boring, happy family," she said, looking at Mallory. "So, we know she hasn't run away. Someone must have taken her. I wish there was another possible reason for her disappearance, but we know there is none." Crying harder, Paul put his arm around his wife, looking very close to tears himself.

"I am so sorry…" Mallory begun, but didn't have the words to finish the sentence.

"And now those bodies have been found. Every time the phone rings or there's a knock at the door, my heart just stops."

After Paul had given Mallory a copy of a recent picture of Harriet and a description of what she wore that day, Mallory left. Feeling her heart breaking for them, she hoped they were wrong, and that Harriet had run away, and would be home soon with her tail between her legs.

Once she was back in the car, she took a few moments to let everything sink in. Driving back to the ranch, Mallory prayed Harriet wasn't one of the bodies, waiting to be identified at the Medical Examiner's office.

"Where are you, Harriet?" Mallory asked the empty car. "What happened to you?" None of it made any sense. She hadn't been booked in the ranch's diary, but her parents believed she was going riding, like she normally would have done at the weekends. She never got on the bus, and there was no video footage of her captured anywhere else. Because of her social anxieties, Harriet had no friends she could have gone out with, and she wasn't speaking to anyone online… Something must have happened while she was waiting for her bus, Mallory thought. But that still made no sense why she wasn't booked in at Elm-Green Farm. It was like she hadn't planned on riding that day. But where could she have gone?

Still feeling troubled when she arrived back at the ranch, Mallory felt like visiting the horses, hoping to clear her mind and overthrow her gloomy mood. Heading into the house, intending to change her clothes, knowing her black heels and pencil skirt really weren't the most appropriate things to wear for her walk to the stables. She went straight up the stairs, hoping no one would think her rude, but the house sounded quiet and there had been no chihuahua alarm, so was sure no one would notice anyway.

Changing into some jeans and ankle boots, she gave her hair a quick brush and reapplied her lip gloss. Grabbing her jacket before leaving the room, she made her way back down the stairs. After poking her head through the kitchen doorway, she could smell a chicken roasting in the oven, but the room was otherwise empty. Exiting the house, she began her walk on the grass up towards the stables. There was a slight breeze in the air, which made Mallory pull her jacket around her tighter.

The Rileys' land was extensive, separated into sections with two or three horses in each of the paddocks, grazing on the grass. It was so quiet out here, so peaceful. She could understand why Harriet loved it here. Straining her eyes, and looking into the distance, she thought she could see Noah and Bobby working on the fence. Walking over to the main paddock closest to the stables, she leaned against the fence and watched the horses having their turn of running around the enormous field.

Sighing, her mind wandering back again to the Dolans. She couldn't imagine what it must be like to lose a child. It had been bad enough losing a mother, without the added feeling of guilt a parent must get from failing to protect their child.

Hearing a sound from behind her, she turned to see Aiden walking with a wheelbarrow toward the stables.

"Mallory," he said with a curt nod.

"Aiden," she said back, just as rigid.

"Busy, are you?" Aiden asked with a sarcastic smile.

Before she could respond, he added, "I'm now going to muck out some stables. Care to help? Of course not. Wouldn't want you to get your fingernails dirty!"

She really was not in the mood for Aiden's poor attitude, she stepped away from the fence and turned around to glare at him. But he had already walked into the stables.

Storming after him, she took off her jacket and hung it by the horses' bridles.

She had really had enough of this man's bullshit. Grabbing a shovel, she followed him into one of the horse enclosures and began shoveling the dirty hay into the wheelbarrow.

Not saying a word to each other, they worked in silence until the enclosure was empty. Lifting the wheelbarrow up, before Aiden could get there, she pushed it out of the stables and headed to where the muck heap was. Working on pure adrenaline, Mallory knew her body wouldn't be thanking her later, but at this point, she did not care.

It would be good to have a workout, she told herself; it was something she would always shy away from, much preferring to read a book in comfort rather than to exercise in a gym.

Tipping the dirty hay onto the mound, she walked the wheelbarrow back to the stables to repeat the job. It didn't take them long before the stables were all clear, neither of them breathing a word to each other.

Walking the wheelbarrow back for the last time, she parked it next to the stable door, picked up her jacket and began walking back towards the house.

"Mallory," he called after her.

Spinning around, she glared at him.

"Thank you."

Mallory nodded at him, turned back around, and when he could no longer see her face, she broke out into a big smile, knowing she had finally cracked Aiden's ice.

Well, she hoped she had because if not, the next time she lifted a shovel, it wouldn't be to shovel horse shit. She giggled to herself.

CHAPTER TEN

Climbing into the truck, he could feel something vibrating and protruding underneath him.

Reaching down, he pulled the offending item out. He couldn't believe his luck!

He had been following his new conquest for days now and this baby was going to make the take a lot easier.

He was certain once he had finished and destroyed the evidence, there would be no tracing back.

Looking into the rear-view mirror, he grinned to himself.

"It's like it was meant to be." He began to whistle as he started the engine.

***

It was a cloudier day today, and Cole and Noah were chatting away in the front of Cole's truck, on their way to the press conference.

Mallory sat in the back seat; her mind occupied. Still wondering why Noah had been a no-show to his own family's welcome home dinner last night. It had been awkward sitting at the kitchen table, eating a delicious roast chicken dinner without Noah's attendance.

She had felt sorry for Susan, who had obviously gone to a lot of trouble making the meal for Noah, and he hadn't even bothered to turn up!

Another surprise was not one of the Rileys' had reacted to Noah not being there. It was almost like they had expected it!

When they had finished the meal, followed by a delicious warm apple pie with homemade ice-cream, Cole and Mallory both offered to clear the kitchen. When they were on their own, she looked at Cole questioningly.

"Don't ask, Mal," he said, and had just shaken his head sadly.

Nothing else was said.

It must be a common occurrence, which was so strange. Noah, Aiden, and Cole seemed so close. But Noah and his parents? Not so much. Something must have happened, her inquisitive mind thought. The journalist in her promised to find out.

The lake was just as busy as it had been the last time they were there. Parking the truck, they started making their way over to where the press had gathered.

"Hey Riley! What you doing here?" a voice shouted, causing both Noah and Cole to turn back.

Seeing Elijah standing with another police officer in uniform, the three of them walked over.

"I'm just making sure you boys are behaving," Noah said as they got closer. Giving both the men handshakes, which quickly turned into bear hugs.

"When did you get back?" Elijah asked, smiling.

"Late Saturday night," Noah said, giving Mallory a wink.

"Ah! You up for beers later then? I think we're going to need them after this shift!"

"Sure, over at Flanagan's?"

"Obviously."

"We will see you there then," smiled Noah.

They walked over to the platform where everyone was waiting for the County sheriff to arrive.

"I take it you're both wanting to meet the guys later for beers?" Noah asked them.

"Sure," Cole said, blushing. Mallory blinked. Had she just imagined that?

"Thought you might," Noah said with a smile. "Mallory?"

"Absolutely. It would be great to ask Eli a few more questions."

Noah frowned, picking up on her coldness to him.

Noticing the crowd was quietening, they looked over to the platform to see the Sheriff had arrived.

"Good morning. Thank you for joining us again today. With a very heavy heart, we can confirm the bodies recovered from Lake Anwar are those of twenty-two-year-old Phoebe O'Neil. Nineteen-year-old Alison Kelly. And twenty-year-old Leilah Wyatt." Pausing, the Sheriff looked up from his speech.

"The families have all been informed, and I trust you will respect their privacy at this extremely troublesome time. Our hearts go out to them, and we share in the grief of their losses." Looking back down at his notes, he carried on.

"We still have our Search and Rescue teams combing the section of the lake, and they will remain doing so until we feel confident enough there is nothing more to be found," Addressing the news cameras again, the Sheriff said firmly.

"Anyone with any information, must come forward. We are treating this as a homicide case and we will not rest until we have the person or persons responsible, in our custody. Thank you."

"Sheriff, are you treating these victims as a connected case?" a man from the front asked.

"I'm not able to go into detail, but the evidence so far suggests they are linked."

"Sheriff! Do you know how long the bodies had been down there for?" a woman closer to the front asked.

"The bodies were in different stages of decomposition, which brings us to believe they had been killed at varying times. However, the results from the autopsies, and the proximity of the bodies' locations, suggest they were placed in the water at the same time."

"Sheriff! Are you expecting to find any more bodies in the lake?" asked another journalist.

"We certainly hope not, but at this stage we are ruling nothing out." he said, looking around and nodding to a man with his hand up, "last question."

"Are you expecting to find young Harriet Dolan, who is still missing?"

"We are still hoping Harriet Dolan's disappearance is not connected to this case." Nodding to the crowd, the sheriff stepped down from the platform and walked back toward the cordoned area.

"Bloody hell!" Cole exclaimed, as Mallory paused her Dictaphone and looked at him sadly.

"I know, those poor families," she said, feeling a strong sense of relief for the Dolans, especially now she had met them, and witnessed their pain. Then felt incredibly sad, knowing these young women's families would be just as broken-hearted, knowing it was final. Their sisters and daughters would never come home again. And in Phoebe O'Neil's case, a child who would never know his mother.

Feeling dumbstruck, the three of them walked back towards the truck.

"I just can't believe we have a serial killer this close," Cole said, shaking his head.

"It's not great, is it? I'm sure that our boys will find him soon though," said Noah, opening the truck and getting into the driver's side.

The three of them were quietly lost in their own thoughts on the drive back to the ranch.

The clouds were parting after the recent miserable weather, and it looked like the rest of the day was going to be fine and sunny.

After arriving back at Elm-Green Farm, they got out of the truck, and Noah told them he was heading to the stables to take his horse, Maverick, for a hack. Cole decided he would join his brother. Mallory wished she could too, but with today's press conference to write up before the deadline, she was tight on time. She also wanted to finish her article on Harriet now she had received the green light from Monica for her 'still missing girl' news pitch.

"You guys have fun," she said regretfully.

"See you later for drinks," said Noah, giving her a smile that made her feel warm and excited, and making her forget she was pissed at his no show last night.

She opened the door and called out her hello, to no answer. Walking into the empty kitchen, she grabbed herself a coffee and walked upstairs to write her articles.

After feeling satisfied with what she had written, she pressed send. Closing down her laptop, she lay back on her bed and looked out of the window. Her mind drifting back to Noah, wondering if they were still out riding. She imagined he looked captivating on his horse. Big, strong, and charming. She sighed, wondering what color his horse was, picturing Maverick to be dark brown, with a golden sheen when the light hit him at the right angle, which would match Noah's eyes and hair coloring perfectly...

Shaking her head, she picked up her phone to call Teresa. Unfortunately, it rang through into voicemail, so she left a brief message to tell her to buy the newspaper tonight. The bodies had been identified.

Walking into the bathroom to draw a bath, she poured lots of bubbles into the running water and went to search through her clothes and decide what to wear; she felt like a teenager getting ready to go on a first date.

"Comfortable and casual," she said to herself, "And very cute." Choosing a smart pair of skinny black jeans with a low-cut black top that showed off her cleavage perfectly. With her DMs and green army-camo jacket to finish, it would suit the look she wanted to portray. She smiled.

Sinking into the bath, she put the washcloth on her face and closed her eyes. Relaxing in the hot water and thinking about today's earlier press conference, and then onto Noah, and how he made her feel. Before meeting him, she couldn't even remember blushing. But in the last few days, it was all she seemed to do!

Dipping her head in the bath, she laid emersed in the water until she had to take a breath. She knew she was physically attracted to Noah. She just hoped it wasn't so obvious to everybody else!

Stepping out of the bath, she walked back into the room and got ready. Drying her long black hair, she decided to leave it down; it had finally grown to a length she was happy with. Perfectly applying her make-up and getting dressed, Mallory decided to wear her favorite perfume too, telling herself it had nothing to do with Noah Riley.

Walking downstairs and into the kitchen, Noah, Aiden, and Cole were sitting at the breakfast bar, each with a bottle of beer in their hand. The three of them looked so breath-taking, sitting there, completely oblivious to her presence. All so different in looks and personality, but complementing each other perfectly. Noah laughed at something Aiden had said when Mallory finally caught the eye of Cole.

"Ah, there she is," he said, just as Noah looked up and stopped laughing, his eyes burning into her own. She felt herself blushing. Again.

"You ready boys?" Noah asked his brothers, his eyes not leaving hers. Both of the men agreed and got up, walking towards the front door.

"Looking good, Mal," Cole complimented her and giving her a wink. Even Aiden graced her with a small smile as he walked past. Mallory felt glued to the spot she was standing on as Noah drained the rest of his beer.

"After you, ma'am," he smiled.

Determined not to show his smile was affecting her, she turned and walked out of the front door too.

Spotting Cole in the back of one of the parked trucks, she walked over and got in next to him, while Noah took the front passenger seat next to Aiden. As they drove past Lake Anwar, Flanagan's was another ten minutes away, and the boys began talking about today's earlier press conference.

"I wonder if they have found any more bodies," Cole said. "How long do you think they will search for?"

"Another few days, I expect. Hopefully Eli will know a bit more," Noah said, just as Aiden pulled into Flannigan's car park.

"Be good, kids," smiled Aiden as they opened their doors to get out.

"You not coming in for one?" Noah asked him.

"If you are still here when I'm driving back, maybe I'll drop in for one. Someone's got to drag your drunk asses back home. I'll call you."

"He's seeing his lady friend again," Cole said to her. "It must be getting serious now."

Aiden laughed at him as Mallory and Cole left the car to join the others in the pub.

CHAPTER ELEVEN

Pulling up outside his playpen, he quickly unlocked the padlock, opened the door and walked around to the back of the truck.

Removing the cover, he picked up the body of his new toy, still unconscious from the drugs he had injected, and carried her in.

Walking over to the coffin at the far end of the room, he opened it and placed her in the box.

Untying her hands and feet, he removed the temporary gag he had placed around her mouth, in case the drugs had worn off before he was ready for them too.

Taking off her shoes, he began unbuttoning her jeans, pulling them over her hips and dragging them over her ankles. She had a sexy white lacy thong on that looked mouth-watering over her tanned skin. The little minx!

He was in two minds, whether he wanted to take her underwear off yet. She had obviously been expecting a fun night tonight, and it seemed a waste if she didn't get one.

Removing her flowery top and revealing her white matching bra underneath, he cupped her breast and gave it a hard squeeze. Oh yes! He was definitely looking forward to this one.

Bending down and biting her hard, he soon pulled away; he really must be careful! Knowing that he would be sharing this one and not wanting to ruin her just yet.

Undoing his jeans, he began stroking himself with one hand, while his other was feeling under her thong. It didn't take long for him to finish, shooting all over her face.

He stood back with a smirk and admired his handy work. She was a beauty, and he couldn't wait for them to enjoy her!

Doing up his trousers, he gave her breast a last squeeze before closing the coffin, tightening the chain, and locking the two padlocks.

Smiling to himself, he walked away. Knowing he would be back real soon.

***

"The search equipment looks for an image that matches a body that has drowned in the water, and the position it holds after it has fallen. When their feet hit the bottom, the knees buckle, and the body floats on its back, chest facing the surface, with their arms outstretched. Bit like the Matrix, when ole Keanu is dodging bullets," said Elijah, posing the position, while Noah drank another mouthful of his fifth bottle of beer.

"What I don't understand is, why didn't the inner gases bring the bodies up to float?" Noah asked. "Had he weighted them down?"

The question completely dragged Mallory's attention away from Cole, who was playing pool with the other officer she now knew to be Jamie. Understanding now why Cole had blushed earlier at the press conference, as she sat observing the long, private looks the two men would give each other when the other wasn't looking. Smiling to herself and taking another sip of her Jack and Coke, she looked at Noah and Elijah.

"Well, between us. And it really must be between us." Elijah glanced her way, tipsy. "The bodies had all been found cut open. Completely gutted out. All organs missing," he said with a low voice, while gesturing towards his own chest. "Then the sick fucker refilled the bodies with rocks, and sewn them back up again. Wrapped heavy-gauge chicken wire around their bodies, before throwing them in the lake." Taking a long swig from his bottle of beer, he added, "So they never floated, because there were no gases to bring the bodies back up." Elijah explained, while Noah looked at his long-time friend grimly.

"The sick fuck definitely knew what he was doing then."

"A-ha," Elijah nodded.

"Do you think he's been using other lakes?"

Elijah looked shocked and more than a little disturbed after hearing Noah's question.

"I really hope not. But until we get another report like your bro rang in, we wouldn't have the budget to just go around checking."

"Why do you think it's a man?" Mallory asked, feeling a little more than tipsy.

"Too much muscle needed to be a woman," said Noah. "Alone anyway."

The three of them sat back, lost in their own thoughts for a moment, before Elijah stood up, excusing himself and going to the washroom.

"I might put some music on," Mallory said, looking towards the jukebox. "What sort of music do you like?"

"Rammstein, Five Finger Death Punch, Stone Sour," he said and smiled. She nodded at him, agreeing with his band choices, making his smile grow wider.

Standing up, she walked over to the jukebox, digging in her pockets, searching for loose change. Slotting the coins into the machine, she looked through the selections. It offered none of the bands he had listed on the playlist. She frowned, but it soon turned into a big smile, when she spotted Black Stone Cherry and Saliva on there. Typing in the codes for her favorite songs, Mallory walked back to the table, a satisfied smile on her face when the first song played.

Noah sat watching her and smiling, while at the bar, Elijah was standing and waiting to be served.

"You're pretty amazing, you know that, right?"

"Black Stone Cherry?" she asked, blushing. "They were the last band I saw back home. They put on an amazing show! Have you seen them?"

"Actually, no, I haven't seen any live music in a long time. Can never get the tickets, not knowing exactly when I'll be back home."

"Yeah. That must suck!" she blurted out without thinking. She really must slow down drinking now. But it only made Noah laugh at her.

"Yes, it does."

"How long do you think you will be a Devil Dog for?" she asked him, using the slang name for the Marines.

"I don't know. I can't imagine myself doing anything else," he admitted. "Once a Marine, always a Marine." He smiled.

Mallory realized the whole time they had been speaking, they had both gradually leaned closer to each other to hear over the music. If she just moved a little closer, their noses would touch. Blushing wildly, Mallory moved back in her seat, casually looking around to check that no one had noticed. She didn't have to worry. Cole was too busy talking and playing pool with Jamie to notice them, and Elijah was busy balancing everyone's drinks on the tray to bring them over. She best make that her last one, before she embarrassed herself by doing something stupid, like climbing onto Noah's lap!

Looking up at him to see if he had noticed her reaction, she could have sworn he had an almost disappointed look on his face by her moving away.

"There you go, Mallory."

"Thank you, Eli," she smiled and accepted another JD and coke. "This really must be my last one. If not, I have no chance of making it to tomorrow's press conference."

"Luckily, I'm off duty tomorrow," Elijah said, nodding over to the boys, who had just racked the balls up again for another game. "Those two look like they are still going strong."

"I'll give Aiden a call and see if he's heading our way soon," Noah said, retrieving his phone out of his pocket.

"So, Mallory, how long do you think you will stay at the Rileys for?" Elijah asked her.

Thinking for a moment, she answered him, "Maybe for another week. All depending on if they arrest someone soon, I guess. I don't honestly know. I'm pretty new to all of this." It was a manhunt now, and hopefully the police would have someone in custody soon. She looked over at Noah, who had a frown on his face.

"Makes you and me both," Elijah said. "It really hasn't been that long since I left the academy. This is my first serial killer case, too. I just hope we catch the bastard soon."

"He's not answering," Noah announced, a bit gruffly. "I'll try him again in a little while. If not, I'll call us a taxi."

The conversation soon turned to football, and Mallory watched the men talk. Sports really wasn't her thing, but she enjoyed watching Noah's face turn animated as they spoke about their mutual team. Trying Aiden's phone again, but with no luck, Noah shook his head and then called for a taxi.

"You heading home too?" he asked Elijah.

"Nah, the night is still young man! I'll join the boys. Play the winner."

"You can stay too if you like? I'm a big girl," she smiled.

"No way. Not with some crazy madman on the loose. It's okay, I have had little sleep recently, anyway. I can catch up with these losers anytime."

"Yep! He needs to get home and get some beauty sleep, so he won't feel so bad next time he comes out with the boys." Elijah grinned at them.

Standing up and going to the ladies' room, her thoughts stayed on Noah, which is all they seemed to do since meeting him again. Mallory knew she was in trouble! But what she didn't know was if it was the greatest of ideas to take things further. She lived hundreds of miles away from the ranch, and he was in the Marines after all.

Stepping out of the cubicle and walking over to the basins to wash her hands, looking in the mirror, she reapplied her lip gloss. Mallory had never considered being involved with someone who was in the services before. Would she be able to handle that, she wondered. Not being able to see him for months at a time and not knowing where he was, or even if he was safe. Noah didn't seem the type that you could just sleep with and forget in a hurry.

And would he even be interested in starting something with her, anyway? All she knew was, when he was in the room, she couldn't help but stare. When he was close, she felt a heavy tension between them, and she was sure he must feel it, too. She wanted to touch him. To feel if his skin was as smooth and warm as it looked… No! The best thing would be to just stay friends and save herself from the heartache.

Giving herself a stern look in the mirror, she walked back into the bar area. Noah and Elijah had joined Cole and Jamie up at the pool table, the four men laughing.

"Someone ordered a taxi? It's outside," the barman shouted.

Saying bye to the boys, Cole decided as he had nothing to get up for the next day, he would stay out longer. Mallory and Noah walked outside for the taxi.

"Are you sure you don't want to stay out too?" Mallory asked Noah.

"Positive," he said, smiling down at Mallory. Making her want to forget everything she had just promised herself in the washroom!

***

Once they had arrived back at the ranch, Noah told the taxi driver to pull up at the gate, and they would walk the rest of the way to the house. Normally, the idea of walking through the trees and down Elm-Green Farm's drive at night would have filled her with horror. But walking with Noah, she felt safe, and when he reached down to hold her hand, she wished they had further to walk.

His hands were huge in her own, warm and soft. Just as she imagined they would be.

"Noah, can I ask you a personal question?" she asked, feeling brave.

"Sure."

"Why didn't you attend Susan's welcome home dinner yesterday?" She could feel him tense up.

"Can I answer that another time?" Noah asked, stopping to look at her.

"I guess so. Sorry I asked, I didn't want to upset you."

"You didn't. I just don't want to ruin tonight by talking about my parents," he said bluntly, making her curiosity flair.

"Mallory, can I ask you a personal question?"

"Sure," she grinned.

"What would you do if I kissed you?" Her grin slipped and her breathing stopped.

He pulled her closer. Wrapping her in his arms and lowering his face until their lips met. Softly groaning, he deepened the kiss. Their lips parting, and their tongues slowly meeting, stroking each other.

She didn't know how long they stood there like that. Time no longer existed. Only Noah did. With his arms around her, tasting and becoming familiar with the way they both moved their mouths in harmony with each other. She tingled all over.

When he pulled away, they were both panting.

"I've been wanting to do that since you turned on the light and had a gun pointed at my head," he whispered, brushing a strand of her hair away and tucking it behind her ear.

Holding hands, they walked the rest of the way to the house. Noah unlocked the door, and they walked up the stairs together.

Once they were at Mallory's door, he pulled her to him, desperate to claim her mouth again. He hungrily kissed her. She didn't want him to stop. As the kiss grew more intense, she tried to pull him into her room. Suddenly desperate to feel all of him. But he gently shook his head, looking at her regretfully. Knowing if she pushed the matter, she could get him to change his mind. He groaned and cupped her face with his hands.

"Please don't look at me like that, Mallory," he whispered. "You don't know how hard it is for me to walk away right now." Giving her another soft, quick kiss on the lips. He gave her one last look, turned around, and walked back down the stairs.

Leaving Mallory alone in the hallway. Her heartbeat pounding and her body throbbing.

CHAPTER TWELVE

"Soon, I will remove your gag," he said, giving this new pretty toy a friendly smile.

"We are in an isolated area. Miles away from anyone, and my playpen has been soundproofed, so it really is pointless to scream."

Moving closer to the blonde beauty, strapped in his special chair, he whispered like he was sharing a secret, "and screaming irritates the fuck out of me. There is a time and a place for screams, and that is usually after punishments."

Watching while she squirmed, a panicked look on her face. He told her matter-of-factly, "and one reason for receiving punishments is screaming unnecessarily. I don't give second chances. I will put the ball gag back in your mouth and keep it in there at all times. Only remove it when it is time for you to eat or suck. Do you understand?"

Nodding, with her eyes wide open, he leaned over and removed the ball gag from her mouth.

"Anytime you need to shit or piss, tell me and I will take you. I am not here to clean up your shit. If you lie, you will be punished. Do you understand?"

Nodding, she whispered in a croaky voice, "where are my clothes?"

"For what you're going to be used for, clothes will only be in the way," he said, smiling again at her, watching as big silent tears dripped from her face.

"And your mouth is for sucking, not talking. Heed this warning, if you use your teeth as a weapon, I will cut your nipples off and make you eat them. If it's deemed a bad bite, I will cut off your breasts."

"Just like all the toys before you, people will be looking for you, search parties out hunting." Giving her a mock sympathy look.

"But nobody's going to come and look for you here. So just accept your fate."

***

Walking nervously down the stairs the next morning, Mallory really didn't know what to expect. She had spent the night tossing and turning, and hoping Noah would change his mind and come back into her room. With no such luck!

The kitchen was silent as she walked in to get her coffee. Not even Susan was in there. Mallory double checked the time, making sure she wasn't late getting up.

Taking a cup and filling it with coffee, she grabbed a croissant from the plate that was loaded with pastries left by the coffeepot and sat at the breakfast bar. Maybe Susan had an appointment this morning, she thought to herself, looking out of the kitchen window.

"Good morning, Mallory," Noah said, making her jump as he walked in. His hair still damp from the shower he had obviously just taken, making his hair look even darker. He really should come with a warning label, she thought, smiling her greeting.

"Sleep well?" she asked him.

Looking straight at her, he replied, "No. Not really." Pouring himself a coffee, "did you?" he asked, spooning sugar into his cup.

"No. Me neither." She blushed.

"Please stop blushing, Mallory. It makes me want to drag you upstairs and finish what we started last night."

Not knowing what to say and turning even redder. Mallory gulped her coffee down, burning her throat.

"Where is everyone?" she asked him when she could trust her voice again.

"It seems like Aiden and Cole didn't come home last night. And who knows where the parents are? Sometimes they will go out for breakfast if they haven't got a lot on."

"So, it's just us then?" Mallory asked. Then swallowed, noticing the look in Noah's eyes in reaction to her question.

"I'm going to go wait in the truck for you. If not, we won't make this morning's conference." he said, his eyes burning into her own.

She nodded and stood up. Putting her cup and plate in the dishwasher.

"You're coming too? You know I have my car here, don't you?"

"Of course. While we have a crazy person taking girls randomly, do you really think I could let you go by yourself?"

Walking towards the front door, he suddenly pulled her back and kissed her again like he was a starved man. Tasting like coffee and toothpaste, she ran her hands down his firm chest, wishing she didn't need to adult, and attend this morning's press conference.

Groaning, he let her go, looking at her and shaking his head.

"We'd better leave now," he said, and she laughed at him. "Oh, you think it's funny, do you?" And chased her out of the house.

Just as they were getting into the truck, they noticed Cole was walking up the drive. Driving up to him, Noah slowed and wound down his window.

"Good morning, baby brother. Did you have a good night?"

"Yeah," he said, smiling and looking sheepish.

"Well, you have the house to yourself, so you will have no one else to witness your walk of shame." Noah grinned at him.

"Swell," Cole said, looking exhausted. "Aiden not home yet?"

"Nope, not yet. Seems like he had a crazy night too."

Cole grinned up at his brother as Noah wound his window back up and drove to the gate. Mallory hopped out, opened it, and got back in after he had driven through.

"I wonder if they have found any more bodies," she said, looking out of the window to another sunny morning.

"Let's hope not," Noah replied grimly. "Hopefully, they have found the killer, or have the leads to be getting closer to an arrest."

Mallory nodded in agreement. "Do you think it's someone local?"

"I'll be surprised if it isn't. You wouldn't want to be transporting those bodies for miles, would you?"

"It's such a shame that the lake has no video surveillance."

"Yeah. Even if it was just at the entrances," agreed Noah.

Parking up on arrival, they both got out of the truck and slowly made their way over to the normal gathering place, where an enormous crowd had already formed. Each day, there seemed to be more people in attendance, as the case was gaining more media attention.

"Good morning. Thank you for joining us on our fourth day of investigations. Our Search and Rescue have been working tirelessly around the clock since first attending Lake Anwar. We have had the help of diving teams and water cadaver dogs. As well as the use of specialized sonar equipment and aqueous drones, in the help of scouring a large section of the lake, where the bodies were originally recovered." Looking up from his notes, the County Sheriff scanned the sea of faces of the press.

"Thankfully, I can report, they have detected no other bodies since the first initial recoveries. We are now satisfied that there is nothing untoward left to discover, so we will end the search of the lake." Looking directly at the video cameras of the local news station, he added, "However, despite our exhaustive inquires, the circumstances around the victims' disappearances and untimely deaths are still unclear to us, and are still subject to our ongoing investigations. You must come forward with any information, big or small. The families of the victims have set a cash reward for any information which leads to a conviction. This person and anyone else involved in these horrendous murders are very dangerous. And we must have them in our custody before they can attack again. Please contact your local police department. Be very vigilant, stay in groups, and do not travel alone."

Walking away, and feeling relief that no other bodies had been found at the bottom of the lake, but concerned the police still didn't have a suspect, Mallory and Noah got back in the truck.

"I never realized they could use cadaver dogs for underwater cases," said Mallory, buckling her seatbelt.

"Uh-huh," Noah nodded, turning the ignition. "Apparently, they can pick up the scent of a body, up to thirty meters underwater. They can even detect the difference between human and animal remains."

"That is amazing!"

"Definitely. They really are invaluable to the search crews; I would bet good money on them being the main reason the search only took four days. The dogs' stamina really is incredible. They just keep working until they find something," said Noah, driving away from Lake Anwar.

Mallory asked him if they used cadaver dogs in the Marine Corps. He was clearly knowledgeable about the subject.

"Oh yeah, in the Corps we have multi-purpose dogs. A friend of mine trains them, actually. Familiarizing them with the sounds of gunfire, and everyday noises they would experience in the military, such as the rappelling of helicopters."

Watching him talk, she couldn't imagine Noah's everyday life in the Marines.

"They even have the dogs riding Zodiac boats and sky-diving."

"Wow!" she exclaimed, "I don't even think I could jump out of a plane."

"I used to hate it," Noah said with a grin. "But after my fourth or fifth jump, I got over my fear and I'm used to it now. Before then, I would need physically pushing out!" He laughed.

Mallory looked out of the window, thinking about how dramatically different their lives were. She was a greenhorn journalist, still living at home with her father, and he was a military man, traveling the world and experiencing situations she couldn't even imagine. She must seem so boring to him!

"Do you have anything planned for the rest of the day?" asked Noah, as they drove back up the drive towards the ranch house.

"Not after I have written today's article. No."

"Would you like to go for a ride? Maybe take a picnic?" he asked with a small smile.

"That sounds fantastic," she said, making his smile grow.

"Great. Meet me at the stables when you're ready. I'll saddle up the horses. Roxy is your ride, isn't she?"

"Yes please, she is beautiful."

They both stepped into the still, silent house. Hercules woke up from his little bed in the kitchen, looking very pleased to have some company. He ran over to greet them. Mallory picked him up and stroked his head while he tried to give kisses to her face.

"Ah, you're cute, Herc, but not that cute." Mallory laughed, dodging his tongue.

"Coffee Mallory?"

"Please."

"I'll bring it up for you, if you want to make a start on your article," Noah said with a frown, "the pot is empty."

Mallory had been staying at Elm-Green Farm for over a week now, and it was the first time a pot of coffee wasn't ready for drinking. Susan couldn't have been home yet.

"Thanks Noah, you're a star."

Putting Hercules down, she walked up the stairs, followed by the tiny dog. Sitting at her normal position on the bed, she opened her laptop and smiled when Hercules jumped up next to her, and made himself comfortable on the bed.

She had already begun typing when there was a soft knock on her door.

"Come in."

Noah opened her bedroom door, holding a cup of fresh smelling coffee. Looking up at him, she couldn't help but wish he had entered her room a few hours ago. Feeling herself blushing again, she thanked him and looked back down at the screen.

"See you in an hour or two." he smiled as he left her room.

Watching the door close, she sighed dreamily. "Oh, get a grip Mallory!" she said when she realized she was still staring at the closed door. "You're acting like a teenager!"

Hercules looking at her with a confused expression.

"Not you, sweetheart," she told him, stroking his head. "I'm talking about me. I'm twenty- four and acting like I've never even seen a man before!"

Shaking her head, she looked back to the laptop, wanting to hurry and finish, so she could get out of there and go riding with Noah.

"And I have my priorities twisted in all the wrong way!"

Lifting her steaming cup, she blew at it and took a small sip. Looking at the little dog, who seemed to be watching her with a knowing look.

CHAPTER THIRTEEN

He liked to stretch things. It had always fascinated him to see how far their pussies could be pulled open.

Piercing hoops into both of his pretty toy's cunt lips, he threaded nylon cord through, and connected them to rings on both sides of his special chair.

He pulled the cord tight, opening her pussy up.

Her whimpers turning into screams.

"Hush your noise. Both holes between your legs will stretch for me."

Her head began thrashing side to side in panic mode.

"Calm down. It'll hurt a little, but it will stretch. Your pussy is designed for a baby to come out, and we won't be using anything bigger than that." He chuckled.

***

Mallory was full of excitement as she walked up to the stables to meet Noah. As she got closer, she could see Aiden grooming a horse.

"Hey, did you have a good time last night?"

"Not really. Although it did get better," he said, as she stroked the horse's muzzle.

"Met some friends, and ended the night sleeping on their couch. I'm getting too old for that shit though." He moaned, cricking his neck.

Things couldn't have gone too well with his date last night, thought Mallory.

"Noah around?"

Tipping his head toward another stable block, where the Rileys' personal horses were kept, she smiled her thanks and walked over.

Spotting Roxy, who had been saddled up and was drinking from a trough, she went inside. Noah was standing next to a black gelding, grooming him.

"I take it this is Maverick?" she asked, smiling and walking over to them.

"Yes, it certainly is."

"He's gorgeous," she said, holding her hand out so Maverick could smell her before she stroked his forehead.

"He knows." Noah grinned. Placing the saddle and saddlebags onto Maverick's back and securing the straps. Once he had fitted the bridle, he looked at Mallory.

"You all ready? Shall we go to the blocks?" he asked her.

"Please," she smiled. She had never tried mounting a horse without the help of a block before.

Handing Mallory Maverick's reins, they left the stables. Noah walked over to the other horse, untied Roxy, and gave her a sugar lump. Whispering something softly to her as he began walking her to the main stable block.

Aiden left the horse he was tending to and offered to help, taking the reins from his brother and lining Roxy up to the mounting block. Mallory was still getting used to Aiden's new attitude towards her. She much preferred this Aiden!

Once she had mounted Roxy, she looked over to see that Noah was already sitting on Maverick. The image of them took her breath away. They looked so majestic.

"Have fun," Aiden said, walking back to the golden horse he had been grooming.

Following Noah, she trotted Roxy towards a different trail to where she and Cole had gone on her last ride. They were soon cantering towards the mountains. Mallory smiled, feeling the breeze, and enjoying the sense of happiness and freedom riding a horse always gave her.

Twenty minutes later, they entered a forest. Noah slowed Maverick down to a trot, so Mallory could ride Roxy beside them.

"Feeling hungry?"

"Yes," she smiled. Breakfast seemed ages ago, and she had only eaten a croissant.

"We will clear the forest in a moment and be at one of my favorite spots."

It wasn't long before she could see the trees clearing and could hear the sound of running water. As they passed through the clearing, there was a lush green growth of grass next to a narrow stream, the water burbling over the rocks. Mallory smiled; she couldn't think of a more perfect way to spend her afternoon.

"Wow. This is great," she said, watching Noah dismount Maverick and leading him to the stream.

Copying his actions, Mallory gracefully got down from Roxy, knowing she wouldn't be able to get back on as easily, but she would worry about that later!

Opening the saddlebags, he pulled out a picnic blanket and laid it on the grass.

"Ma'am."

"Thank you, kind sir."

Sitting on the blanket, she watched Noah pulling out Tupperware boxes and a small bottle of wine, which he poured into small plastic glasses, and handed her one.

"Wow," she repeated and smiled, "You thought of everything."

"Of course." Sitting beside her and handing her a smoked salmon and cream cheese bagel.

He had set out little containers of strawberries, raspberries and blueberries, along with some carrot sticks and sweet cherry tomatoes, on the picnic blanket.

"This is great. Thank you, Noah."

Sitting in comfortable silence, they ate their lunch, watching the running stream and enjoying the sunshine.

"So, Mallory, what made you want to become a journalist?"

Thinking for a moment, she answered him.

"I liked the idea of being able to talk about issues that are important to me. To educate and bring people the facts. Help to change some misconceptions," she said with a small smile and taking a sip of her wine. "Not that I've been able to do that yet."

Looking at him, she picked a strawberry from the pot. "Hopefully one day, though. What about you? Why did you want to join the Marines?" she asked before biting into the berry.

"Adventure," he said, laying down with his elbow up, resting his head on his hand. "Travel the world. Serve my country." He smiled, "Leave this place."

Copying his actions, she laid beside him and looked at him with a serious expression.

"Why would you want to do that? Don't you love it here?"

"My brothers and the horses? I miss them when I'm deployed. But Thomas and Susan? No. Not really," he admitted, looking her straight in the eyes.

"But why?" Mallory asked, genuinely confused by his answer.

"Growing up, they were a lot harder on me than they were with Aiden and Cole. But then, I always did step up to take their punishments, too. It used to upset me more to watch them get it instead. So, I never felt a close relationship with them, like the boys seem to have."

"What do you mean? They used to beat you?"

"I wouldn't say beat, no. Thomas was always very conscious not to leave any marks. But he was always heavier handed with me, and when he was in his dark moods, we all knew to keep away. But sometimes he would come looking. And I guess I was the one who always spoke up." Looking towards the stream, he added, "Aiden has inherited the same moods, unfortunately. But luckily, he never gets physical with them," Noah said, looking back to Mallory, "as far as I'm aware, anyway."

"And Susan?" Mallory asked, feeling shocked and sad by his revelation.

"She never stepped in, said nothing. Did nothing. She just let him get on with it, and it wasn't out of fear, either. Anyone can see she adores him. It's like she believes if Thomas is doing it, then it's the right way to act. No matter what he does. So, I lost respect for her years ago, too," he said, shaking his head.

"The biggest nail in the coffin for me was after I signed up for the Marines. They expected me to work at the ranch after college. Especially being the oldest, but I knew that life wasn't for me. I needed more than horses." Sitting up, he refilled their plastic glasses while Mallory watched him quietly. Her heart breaking for younger Noah.

She had experienced nothing like he was describing with her own father.

"So, I signed up behind their backs as soon as I turned eighteen," he admitted. "I knew he would do anything to stop me. So, when the time came to tell them, that's when he beat me. Badly. And Susan just stood there, watching."

Mallory gasped, her eyes filling with tears.

"I only come back to see the boys and my horse. If they weren't here, I wouldn't ever come back. Although Thomas would never say or do anything out of line to me now. I've finally grown bigger than he ever was," he told her, smiling sadly. "And he doesn't touch the others either. He's gotten soft in his old age. But the damage is still there for me, and they know it."

Feeling the powerful urge to comfort Noah, she leaned across to him and kissed him on the mouth. He wrapped his arm around her and dug his other hand in her hair, holding her to him. As their kiss deepened, he laid back and pulled Mallory on top of him. Groaning and panting between kisses, they began grinding on each other, wishing that they didn't have the barrier of clothes.

Pulling his face away panting, he gasped. "We need to stop."

Knowing she was doing the right thing, and this is what she wanted, she bravely stood up. Apart from the birds in the trees and their horses, no one could see them. Not taking her eyes from his, she lifted off her top and undid her bra. Noah's eyes turned into liquid fire. Breathing shakily, he asked her if she was sure. Not answering him, but showing him, her pants soon followed.

She stood proudly in front of him, with her long black hair falling down her back, feeling no fear, just desperation for Noah. He gave a low groan, reaching for her and pulling her down next to him on the blanket, where she stayed for the rest of the afternoon.

***

Riding back to the stables, Mallory could not remove the smile from her face. The afternoon really had been exquisite with Noah. The sun on their naked skin, while they kissed and caressed each other, with the sounds of running water drowning out their gasps and moans, and sometimes shouts of pleasure. Their bodies had fitted perfectly together, and Noah had been beyond comparable. He was a beautiful man.

Climbing down from her horse, she thanked Roxy again before leading her to the water trough. A stable hand she hadn't met before walked over to greet them, offering to walk Roxy and untack her. Smiling him a thank you, she handed the young man the reins and walked over to where Noah had dismounted.

"Are you heading back to the house now?"

"Not yet. I just need to walk Maverick and cool him down. I'll catch up with you once I've untacked him."

"Okay," she said, turning and feeling disappointed they were parting after sharing such closeness. Heading to the house, she promised herself a nice long soak before dinner. Feeling happier, she walked into the ranch house, hearing the television on in the kitchen, Mallory walked through with the purpose of saying hello. She hadn't seen Susan all day, but entering the kitchen, she saw it wasn't Susan as she presumed it would be, but Cole and Aiden, both standing and watching the TV.

"Hello boys," she said, with a cheerful tone and a big smile, which soon turned into a frown when she noticed the color had drained from Aiden's face.

Looking over at Cole who was watching the news, he looked at her and spoke.

"They have reported another girl missing."

CHAPTER FOURTEEN

*"**D**on't try anything stupid. If you do, I will slit your throat."*

She nodded quickly, eyeing the bucket of clean water and the sponge he had brought with him.

"I will untie your hands and feet. I don't enjoy stirring my own porridge, so I will let you use the bathroom to wash yourself."

After yesterday's very enjoyable, four-hour playtime with his penetration machine, she needed a clean before he touched her again.

He knew he was a monster. But he wasn't a filthy one.

Leading her to a small section of the playpen where he had installed a toilet, the collar and chain still attached to her neck and hooked around a pole on the ceiling.

"You have exactly five minutes."

Turning his attention to his other toy, he walked over and unlocked the coffin.

He always liked to have a turnaround of at least two girls in his pen, and this one he had kept for a lot longer than usual.

She was one of the youngest toys he had played with. She was never planned, instead an opportunity take.

She had not been a disappointment, instead a pleasant surprise! She had been very hard to break, and he had thoroughly enjoyed his time with her.

He was not finished with her yet. He needed to keep her in a relatively healthy state.

"It's feeding time Harriet. Time to wake up."

***

"What the... What?" Mallory turned her head to watch the news report.

"Freya James, a twenty-four-year-old woman from Portland, was reported missing today after failing to come home last night. She has not been contactable, which her parents claim to be highly unusual. She was last seen leaving

her house for a night out yesterday evening and has not been seen by friends or family since. Jesse Wallis reports."

An image of a beautiful girl, with short blonde, pixie-cut hair and sun-kissed skin, flashed on the screen. While the voice of Jesse Wallis described what Freya was wearing, and the time and place she was last seen.

"Fears have grown quickly, concerning the whereabouts of Freya James, with the gruesome discoveries in the last few days at Lake Anwar, and with another young woman, Harriet Dolan, still missing. Police have circulated Freya's photo quickly; in the hope someone will have some information leading to her whereabouts. There has been a public outcry since the discoveries at Lake Anwar. People are calling for the authorities to do more. The County Sheriff has announced there will be a more visible police presence on the streets of Portland over the coming weeks. He has also reiterated the importance of being vigilant and not traveling alone."

"Oh no," Mallory said.

Without a word, Aiden stormed out of the kitchen, causing Mallory and Cole to turn at his exit.

"What's wrong with him?" asked Mallory.

"Who knows with Aiden?"

At that moment, Susan walked through into the kitchen, both hands full of food shopping bags.

"Who's up for a cook-out tonight?" she asked.

***

Perched on the bed and still wrapped in a bath towel, Mallory was talking to William on her phone, asking if he had seen the recent news report on the latest missing woman.

"It's like he's running rings around the police!"

"Uh -huh. He's certainly brave, or very stupid! And guess what else I found out? But I need to keep it under wraps for now. The sick bastard has been cutting the poor women open and removing all of their organs!"

"What? Why? What's he been doing with their innards?"

"Who knows? Throwing them in the lake separately, I'm guessing. He's doing that so the bodies don't float back up again."

"Ah yes, because of the gasses."

"Uh-huh."

"I guess weighting them down wasn't enough for him. He obviously knows what he's doing." William said, repeating Noah's comment when they had been told.

"He sounds experienced. Or maybe he's in the medical field," Mallory wondered, speaking her thoughts out loud.

"Maybe," William agreed. "Do you know if the police have any leads at all? Fingerprints? Tyre tracks? Surveillance footage?"

"No. As far as I'm aware, they have nothing. Although, they may have information they're not releasing."

Telling William about her meeting with the Dolans, and how seventeen-year-old Harriet had just vanished with no clues or sightings, she listened to William's sympathetic response.

"Those poor parents… I can't even imagine, and I wouldn't want to. Mallory, you must stay safe! And make sure you are with one of the Rileys all the time."

Reassuring her father, she told him either Cole or Noah went with her whenever she left the ranch.

"Good. How are things with Aiden? Has he warmed to you yet?"

"Things are a lot better actually," she said, but then remembered him storming out of the kitchen only an hour ago.

"He's just really moody, Dad. Like slash your tyres moody."

"Oh. Bet he's fun to live with."

Lowering her voice slightly, "Actually, I wanted to ask you, Thomas said you were in the same dorm at college? And after you graduated, he stayed with you for a while until he rented his own place?"

"Yes, that's right. We had some crazy times together." William chuckled.

"Did he ever have mad, dark moods?" asked Mallory, thinking about what Noah had said earlier.

"Thomas? No, not at all." William paused. "If he did, he kept those to himself. He used to spend a lot of time alone in his room, but then again, we were at college. When we weren't drinking and chasing girls, we were there studying."

"Yeah, I guess."

"He's a private man, a lot more introverted than I was, but I would never have described him as moody." He laughed again, then sobered, "Why? Is he moody now too?"

"No, no. Just something one of the boys said about Aiden's moods. That he had inherited them from Thomas," she said, not wanting to break Noah's confidence.

"Anyway Dad, I've got to go. Thomas is cooking a barbeque."

"Okay Mally. Stay safe. Fingers crossed they catch someone soon. The house is getting quiet without you now."

"Had enough of walking around in the nude?"

"Yeah. It's not as good as I thought it would be. I almost gave poor Doris from next door a heart attack when she walked past with her dog."

"Miss you Dad, see you soon."

Still laughing, as she ended the call, she took her towel off her head and got dressed. Thinking back to the latest news report, she pondered if Freya James was another unfortunate victim of the killer, or if she was unrelated to the case. Like everyone else, she hoped young Harriet Dolan was still alive.

She would be surprised if Freya had just gone away for a few days without telling anyone, she would have to be incredibly stupid and selfish if she had, especially as everyone living in Portland must be aware there was a serial killer on the loose, and using their city for a hunting ground! If she was the latest victim, then he really wasn't leaving it long between abductions. Poor Leilah Wyatt had only been taken a couple of weeks ago.

Brushing her hair, she looked in the mirror and wondered why the gaps were getting smaller. Was he getting too confident? Cocky because the police hadn't caught him yet? Was he wanting to get caught, so was being sloppy? If that was the case, then hopefully he would soon lead the police to his arrest.

***

"What would you like to drink, Mal? I'm thinking about cocktails tonight!"

"Ooh yes! That sounds good. What can you make?" Mallory smiled at Cole.

"With help from the internet, all of them."

"How about an Espresso Martini? They are my favorites," Mallory answered him enthusiastically.

"Sounds great," said Cole, typing the drink into his phone's search engine.

"No. Wait," he said disappointedly. "We have no coffee liqueur, damn!"

"How about a Mojito?" she asked him, watching him type the cocktail name in for the ingredients.

"Yes! I think so. Mom, do we have fresh mint?" he asked, looking at Susan.

"Yes, I'll go get some from my herb garden. Make a pitcher, Cole. They sound good!" She laughed, walking towards the side of the ranch house.

"Grab some garlic while you're there. I could use some for the steaks," called Thomas, who was busy lighting the barbeque.

While Susan was busy collecting the herbs, and Cole was in the kitchen preparing the rest of the cocktail's ingredients, Mallory sat back to enjoy the sunset and the beautiful view.

Feeling a scratching on her leg, she looked down at Hercules, wanting some attention. Picking him up and talking to him in a baby voice, Noah walked through. He had obviously showered too, looking fresh in dark blue jeans and a tight fitted white top. Holding a beer, he sat down opposite Mallory and gave her a small, sexy smile.

Trying to hide her obvious reaction to him, she could feel her face flushing. Looking back down at the little dog, she carried on with her cooing. When Hercules saw Susan approaching, he quickly jumped from Mallory's lap to follow her. Great thanks Herc! she thought, having nothing else to occupy herself, and feeling the familiar dancing of butterflies.

After the amazing afternoon they had shared, she didn't know how she should act in front of him. She guessed he wouldn't want the other Rileys knowing of their change in relationship yet, either. It had only just happened, and they hadn't had the chance to have a conversation about keeping things casual, or if they wanted to try something a bit more serious.

Cole walked back out into the garden, carrying two big pitchers of Mojitos, saving Mallory from her awkwardness and making her laugh.

"Wow! After seeing you this morning, I thought your liver might wave a little white flag, after last night's shenanigans."

"I think you may have forgotten; I am a college student Mallory." Cole grinned at her. "This is what we do."

"How silly of me."

"Want one, Noah?" Cole asked as he began pouring the cocktails into glasses full of ice.

"Nah, I think I'll stick to my beer."

"Dad, you want one?"

"I make it a rule not to drink beverages with leaves in," smiled Thomas.

"More for us then, Mal. We can have a pitcher each!"

Walking over with a couple of plates of meat, Susan handed them to Thomas and joined them at the table.

"I'll have one please darling."

"Get your own pitcher!" he said, making Susan laugh as he poured his mother a glass of the minty lime cocktail.

"So, Mallory. When will you need to attend the press conference for the latest missing girl?" Cole asked her.

"What? Another one?" Noah frowned.

Nodding, she relayed the information to him. "It was on the news when I came in after our ride."

"How was it?" Thomas interrupted. "Where did you guys go?"

"We had a picnic by the stream," Noah told him, staring fixedly at Mallory, making her face flush.

"That's nice," Susan said, just as Aiden walked out to join them.

Mallory had never felt so happy to see him as everyone's attention moved to his arrival.

"Aiden! You want a Mojito?" she greeted him enthusiastically, intending to change the subject.

Aiden just screwed his nose up and lifted his beer. He was obviously in another fine mood, Mallory thought.

"Well, I think they are lovely," Mallory said to Cole, smiling and putting her now empty glass down for a refill.

"Me too," said Susan, putting her glass down next to Mallory's with a giggle. Cole refilled their glasses, along with his own.

Everyone was in good spirits, enjoying the food and drinks. Everyone except Aiden, who seemed to have reverted to the Aiden she had encountered on her first days at the ranch.

"Has anyone seen my phone? I can't find the damn thing," he almost growled.

"Do you want me to call it?" asked Cole.

"No, I've tried. The battery must be dead." He left without eating, mumbling about looking upstairs for it again.

Yet again, none of the other family members reacted. They were all obviously very used to Aiden's moods. She was positive nobody on the outside of the Riley circle would believe it, but theirs was quite a dysfunctional family! Wondering if every family of this size was the same, and feeling pleased it was just her and William. Maybe the topic could make a potential future article project. 'The bigger the family, the more dysfunctional the people'; She made a quick note on her phone.

Cole refilled her glass and offered Susan another.

"Oh, no thank you darling. I think it's time for your father and I to go to bed. It's getting late."

Both Thomas and Susan said their goodnights and walked back to the house, hand in hand.

"Want to go inside?" Noah asked Mallory, noticing her shiver.

"Please. It's still quite cool in the evenings, isn't it?" she said, as they picked up their drinks and made their way back into the house.

"Give it another few weeks and it won't be."

Cole switched on the lamps in the big living room as Noah lit the open fire, making the room feel warm and cozy. Mallory made herself comfortable on the sofa and waited for the boys to join her.

Her phone vibrated on the table. Picking it up, she smiled to see Teresa requesting to Face-time. She smiled and accepted the video call. Her best friend's face filled the screen.

"Hey girl, what the actual fuck is happening in Portland? Another one? I can't believe it!"

"Me neither!"

Mallory stood to take the call in another room. As she turned, Teresa spotted Noah on her screen.

"Well, hello there…" Teresa said in her best over-exaggerated, seductive voice. "And who is this fine specimen?" Causing Mallory to blush again. Teresa raised her eyebrows, immediately picking up on Mallory's reaction.

"That would clearly be me." Cole grinned, taking Mallory's phone. "My parents saved all the good looks and charm for their last born."

Mallory could hear Teresa laughing as Cole walked off, proceeding to Face-time with Teresa.

"I apologize for my brother." Noah grinned, pulling her closer. "No, actually I don't. Now I get to have you to myself for a moment," he whispered in her ear, sending goosebumps down her neck and making her breasts tingle.

If Cole's voice hadn't been returning, she couldn't be certain she wouldn't have begged Noah to take her again. Right there. Right then. She turned around just as Cole walked back into the room, busily chatting away and making Teresa laugh. Giving her time to grind her behind on Noah's growing bulge. Making them both groan.

"I'll pass you over to Mallory, she's looking extremely jealous that we are besties now too." Cole grinned, thankfully not noticing the real expression on her face.

Taking her phone back, she looked at her screen. Teresa's eyes widened; she had definitely noticed her genuine expression.

"We need to talk!" Teresa laughed.

CHAPTER FIFTEEN

She knew she was back on the Riley's boat; she could feel the gentle swaying motion underneath her feet.

What she had a problem remembering was why it was so dark. The night was pitch black.

Why were they fishing at night?

"Mallory," a voice called out. She turned around to see Noah. Hadn't she gone fishing with Cole?

"Come here, Mallory. I have something to show you."

Feeling like she was floating over to him, she gave him a big smile and walked into his open arms, feeling safe and warm.

"Look up there," he said, pointing up to the sky.

Mallory gasped. It looked like someone was switching the stars on. Each section of the sky was gradually becoming lighter, glittering with mesmerizing brightness.

"It's beautiful," she breathed out. "Stunning."

Watching the sky display, the stars seemed to be getting bigger, or the world was getting closer, she wondered.

With a big flash, the stars started dropping. Falling from the sky and splashing into the water.

"Oh, no!" she cried. "What should we do?"

Leaving Noah and looking over the side of the boat, she could see the lights of the fallen stars sinking to the bottom of the lake.

"We need to get them out quickly!" she shouted.

She turned around to Noah. But he had vanished. She looked back down over the side of the boat, watching helplessly as some of the stars were ascending back to the surface. She frowned. These stars were starting to look different; she could see them changing shapes and morphing into faces.

Focusing on one of the bright shapes, she could see it was starting to resemble Leilah. She gasped, as the face began to hideously decay.

Looking at a different star, she could see this one was beginning to look like Harriet. Her face twisted in horror and silently screaming back up at her.

Crying, Mallory stepped back away from the side. It horrified her to see the entire lake illuminated with fallen star faces.

Looking down again... she screamed.

She could see her own face. Her own bright light with dead eyes staring back up at her.

***

She sat in the kitchen the following morning, getting her caffeine fix. Mallory checked the time on the big hanging clock again. She was waiting for the breakfast news to begin, hoping for an update on missing Freya. She refreshed her social media accounts again, searching for any progress on the investigations, but nothing had been posted yet.

Walking over to the coffeepot and refilling her cup, she stifled a yawn. She really needed to wake up. She had gotten little sleep after her strange dream last night.

It was just her this morning. Noah had crept out of her room as soon as it had gotten light out, and she was sure he had joined Thomas and Aiden at the stables. She had no clue to where Susan or little Hercules were, and she knew Cole would still be sleeping.

Finally, the news intro began and Mallory quickly sat back on the stool. She had angled perfectly in front of the television. After a few moments, Freya's photo flashed up on the screen.

"Portland Police are seeking public help to locate missing Freya James. A twenty-four-year-old woman, who was reported missing yesterday, after failing to come home after a night out with friends. Her car has been found at one of the many car parks, at Portland's Forest Park, close to where Freya lives with her parents. The local police are setting up teams of volunteers to help search the wooded area. At 5,200 acres, Forest Park is one of the largest urban forests in the United States. There are over forty access points to the park, and the Portland Search and Rescue teams are enabling groups of up to twelve people to search in each of the areas."

She knew what she would be doing today! Placing her empty breakfast things in the dishwasher, Mallory walked up the stairs to change into something more appropriate for walking around in a forest.

She contemplated going alone. She was sure it would be safe searching with the police and rescue crews, but her dad's face flashed in her mind, she would ask Noah if he would like to join her, with his training and experience, no doubt he would be an asset to the search.

Walking out of her room, she put her ear to Cole's door and listened. He was still snoring away, like she had guessed he would be. Knocking on the door firmly, she waited a moment.

"What's the matter?" came a groan.

"It's me, can I come in?"

"Hold up." Another groan.

151

After a moment, she heard Cole's feet padding to his door. He opened it and stuck his head out.

"What's up? Is the house on fire?" he asked, eyes still in slits.

"What? No, silly!" She grinned at him. "I've just seen the news. They have found Freya's car abandoned at Portland's Forest Park."

Blinking and looking confused, she could tell Cole was trying to figure out what she was talking about.

"The missing woman?"

"Yes dopey! They are asking for volunteers to help in the search. I'm obviously going to go. I was planning on asking Noah if he would join me, but just checking to see if you wanted to come too before I left."

"Sure. But I really need a coffee first," he answered, rubbing his face.

"Great! I haven't seen Noah yet to ask him. I'll go up to the stables and check. Gives you time to change out of your SpongeBob pants."

"What? Oh, yeah," he grinned, looking down at himself.

Walking to the stables, Mallory could spot Noah painting the fence of the main paddock. It was a warm day already, and Mallory made a mental note to grab her hat and sunscreen before leaving. It was going to be a hot one!

"Hey."

Looking up from what he was doing, he gave Mallory a big smile. "Well, hello you."

"Have you got a busy day planned?"

"Why? Want to go for another picnic?" he said, making her blush. Again.

"Actually no. But we must do that again soon. I've just seen the news; they have found missing Freya's abandoned car at Portland's Forest Park. They are setting search teams up to cover the area. I'm planning on going to help. Cole's willing to come with me, if you are too busy here to join us?"

"That's okay, the painting can wait."

"That's great!"

Her smile completely vanishing, when she noticed a huge black dog was running full speed in their direction.

"Oh, shit!" cried Mallory, as she instinctively darted behind a laughing Noah.

"Don't be scared. Its only Max. Max stop! Max!"

The big dog halted. Mallory could see it was a ridiculously big German Shepherd.

"Good boy. Have you not met Max yet? He's Bobby's." Noah smiled, stroking the dog.

"No, I've not had the pleasure," she said with heavy sarcasm, still keeping her distance behind Noah.

"He's a good boy. Gentle giant. I'll just put this stuff away and tell Bobby I'm going. Pretty sure Aiden's still giving a class at the moment. I'll meet you back at the house. Come on, boy."

***

After making sandwiches for the three of them, Mallory put them in her backpack, along with bottles of water, apples, candy bars, sunscreen, and insect repellent

"Can you think of anything else?" she asked Cole while they were waiting for Noah to finish getting changed.

"First aid kit?"

"Yes! Good thinking."

"There should be one in the truck. I'll go check," said Cole, taking the backpack with him.

As she quickly typed an update for her dad and Teresa on her phone, Noah walked in.

"Ready to go?" she asked, smiling up at him after pressing send on her phone.

"Not just yet," pulling her close and directing her chin towards him. "Now I am," he said after giving her a long kiss, which left her breathing unsteadily.

Putting her baseball cap and sunglasses on, Mallory followed him out of the house.

Cole was at the rear of one of the trucks with the tailgate down, clearly searching for something. He eventually yelled "got it" as he waved a first aid box in the air before putting it into the backpack.

"All sorted." He smiled, and they all climbed in the truck with Noah driving.

The hour-long journey went quickly, with the three of them laughing and singing along with the radio. Their moods quickly sobered once they had arrived at the National Park, seeing the crowds of police, journalists and volunteers awaiting instructions from the Search and Rescue teams.

They parked the truck and walked over to join them, noticing a helicopter circling above. It didn't take long for them to be organized into a group and after learning of Noah's military background; he was voted foreperson and was issued with a radio and a grid map of the section of forest they were required to search.

Walking through the dense woodland, they each took turns calling Freya's name and listening intently for any answers. They searched for any potential hiding places, or anywhere someone could have had an accident. Or worst-case scenario, where a body could be hidden.

The afternoon heat was hitting them hard. They stopped quickly to refuel with water and candy bars before beginning the loop back to base. So far, they had encountered no signs of Freya.

Falling behind, Mallory fell into step with an older woman in the group.

"I am dreading seeing my sister and telling her we didn't find any sign of her," the woman said, starting to cry.

"You are a relative of Freya's?"

"Her aunt. My sister is completely heartbroken. We need to find Freya and bring her home. I really don't think my sister could carry on living if we don't bring her back," she said, miserably wiping her tears.

"I'm a journalist following the missing women's cases. Would you mind answering just a couple of questions? It might help to piece together what happened to poor Freya."

The woman looked at Mallory, surprised. "I guess so," she sniffed. "If you really think it could help us find her."

"Everything helps," Mallory said, pulling out her Dictaphone from her bag. "Do you mind if I record our conversation?"

Nodding her agreement, Mallory pressed record.

"Sorry, I didn't catch your name? And can you please repeat your relationship to Freya?"

"Jennifer. Jennifer Kent. I am Freya's aunt. Her mother, Amelia, is my sister."

"Thank you. Does Freya have any medical issues you are aware of?"

"Only asthma."

"Does she have any problems with alcohol or drugs?"

"Well, she likes to party. But she's a good girl, and I would be very surprised if she was into anything illegal."

"So, Freya isn't involved in any criminal activity that you are aware of? Sorry I need to ask."

Jennifer shook her head. "No, definitely not."

"Do you know if Freya has any financial troubles?"

"No. She is very sensible with her finances."

"Are you aware of any issues Freya might have with friends or family?"

"I really don't think so. Everyone loves Freya."

"No significant changes in her personal life?"

Pausing for a moment to think, Jennifer answered, "she has been on a few dates with someone recently. None of us have met him yet though. I don't remember his name. But I'm sure Amelia has passed that information onto the police. She would definitely know more; they are very close."

"Do you know of any close friends or colleagues of Freya's I could speak to?"

After Jennifer had listed a few names and their relationship to Freya, they were nearly back at the meeting point.

"Thank you for talking to me. I will contact the people you listed and hopefully we might learn a little more."

"We are just desperate to have her back home." And she began to cry again.

***

Arriving back at the ranch, Mallory broke out into an enormous yawn. She really wasn't used to all the walking they had done.

Climbing out of the truck, it surprised her when Noah put his arm around her.

"Tired? I can run you a bath if you'd like?" and lowering his voice added, "I can come and massage your tired muscles."

She looked over at Cole, who was walking to the house at a distance she was sure he could still hear.

"That sounds good. I just need a caffeine hit first, or I'll fall asleep before the bath is ready," she replied, looking questioningly at Noah, who shrugged in response. He was beginning to not care who knew about them, and even though there were still lots of things to talk about, she was happy to go at his pace.

They were sitting at the kitchen table discussing the search when the doorbell rang.

"I'll answer it," said Cole, walking towards the front entrance.

Taking her boots off, she was rubbing her aching feet, when a frowning Cole stepped back into the kitchen, followed by Elijah in uniform.

"Eli!" Noah greeted his friend, standing up with a confused smile. "Have you just finished your shift? Want a beer?" Noah trailed off, looking even more confused when he noticed there was another police officer standing in the doorway.

"I'm afraid not," Elijah answered, looking apologetically at Noah. "I'm here to speak with Aiden. Is he home?"

"Aiden? I think so. Is there a problem?" Noah asked, just as Aiden walked in from the stables, visibly paling when he saw Elijah and the other officer.

"Aiden? What's going on?" Cole asked his brother.

"Care to step outside with me, Aiden? We just need to ask you a few questions."

"I don't want to talk to you before I speak with an attorney," Aiden said, looking panicked. Causing Elijah to step closer and pull out a set of handcuffs.

"Eli, for Christ's sake! What's this all about?" asked Noah.

"Aiden Riley, we would like you to accompany us to the station and assist in our enquiries regarding the disappearance of Freya James."

"What?" Cole almost shouted.

"What the fuck?" said Noah, walking over to his best friend, who was cuffing his brother.

"Noah. Keep your distance," Elijah warned him. "You have the right to remain silent. If you do say anything, what you say can be used against you in the court of law."

"Seriously? Is this a joke?" asked Noah, not walking any further.

"You have the right to consult with a lawyer and have that lawyer present during any questioning. If you can't afford a lawyer, one will be appointed for you if you so desire."

"Just call Dad, Noah. Get him to sort me out an attorney."

"We have a warrant to search and seize your truck too," said the other officer.

"Which one?" asked Cole, while Noah pulled his mobile phone out to call Thomas.

"All of them," Elijah answered grimly.

CHAPTER SIXTEEN

*"**Y**our eyes are just so pretty. I want to lick them," he said, looking down at his toy.*

"But first I need to keep them open," he told her, while holding up some fishing wire and a needle.

"No, please. I'll keep them open. I promise," she begged.

"Shut your mouth, or the gag's going back in."

He could see she was trying to calm herself. Her body was shaking with racking sobs.

He smiled and whistled cheerfully as he threaded the needle.

Gripping her chin to hold her still, he pierced her eyelid and pulled the line through. Sticking the needle into her eyebrow, he made the first stitch.

Her sobs turning into whimpers with every prick.

Feeling satisfied with his needlepoint skills, he moved onto the next eye.

His mobile phone began to ring, interrupting them. Swearing, he contemplated not answering, but looked at the screen and frowned.

"Hello?"

Listening to the voice on the line, his body filled with rage. Rage and panic.

"Okay, I'll be right there."

Furiously, he looked over at his weeping plaything lying on his special chair.

"I said SHUT THE FUCK UP!" he screamed.

Picking up the white plastic tube he had made into a special kind of dildo, he walked over to her.

Opening her mouth, he shoved the tube deep down into her throat, pushing as deep as he could get it. Pressing the button, the line of spikes released from the pipe, puncturing her throat.

"Shit. Shit. Shit!"

Grabbing his things, he quickly locked up and got into his truck. Wondering how the fuck he was going to get them out of this mess.

***

Mallory drove her little car back from the police station in silence, the atmosphere was thick with tension, their three glum faces lost in their own shock.

Aiden?

Aiden was the killer?

They had found out from Elijah; Freya was Aiden's mystery woman.

She just couldn't believe it. None of this made any sense. Everyone knew Aiden had dark moods, but was he capable of killing? She didn't think so, but the text messages from his phone pointed to a different answer.

"What the fu…?"

"Shit!" Mallory shouted. The full beams catching what seemed to be a naked child, huddled by the side of the road. She slammed on the brakes, and the three of them immediately rushed over.

It was a child. She gasped. It was a very beaten and bloodied body of a young girl.

"Quick, wrap this around her." Noah handed Mallory a blanket he had retrieved from the trunk.

"Harriet? Harriet Dolan?" she asked the young girl, recognizing her from the Dolan's family photos. Covering her in the blanket, the frail girl looked frozen in fear.

"You're safe now sweetheart, let's get you in the car," Mallory said in a soothing tone.

Noah reached over to pick her up and carry her to the car, but Harriet shrunk away.

"Your parents will be so happy to see you," Mallory said, holding out her hand. "Let's not keep them waiting any longer." She smiled.

Harriet's expression reacted slightly when she heard Mallory mention her parents. She lifted her frail arm up and took Mallory's hand. Helping her off the ground, she half lead, half carried Harriet towards the car. Cole held the back passenger door open for them.

"Shouldn't we call an ambulance?" he asked.

"The ranch isn't far away. Let's get her comfortable and then ring them. Get her into some clothes, the poor thing."

Nodding their agreement, they helped to get Harriet in the back seat of Mallory's little car. Mallory sat next to her, with her arms around her, whispering and trying to comfort Harriet, while Noah drove the mile back to the ranch.

This time, Harriet let Noah carry her into the house. She was barely conscious and they could all tell she wouldn't be able to walk any further.

Mallory ran upstairs to get her something warm to wear. They had found Harriet! She was so giddy she couldn't think straight. Rushing back down, Mallory walked into the living room, where Noah had laid her down on the sofa, covering her with a blanket.

Cole walked in, carrying a glass of water for Harriet. "I'll ring Jamie now," he said, just as his phone rang in his hand. Frowning he accepted the call.

"What? Oh shit! We will be right there!" Hanging up the phone, he looked at Noah with wide eyes. "It's all happening now! There's a fire in one of the stables. Some of the horses are going crazy."

"Shit. You two go before it gets any worse. I can call 911."

Nodding, Noah gave her a quick kiss and followed his brother out towards the stables.

Walking over to a curled up and beaten Harriet, Mallory sat next to her and gave her some water.

"Don't be scared, sweetheart, you're safe now. My name's Mallory, and we are going to get you back home to your mom and dad. They have missed you so much." She stroked her hair gently. "Are you in any pain?"

Harriet shook. Her eyes like screaming pits of horror.

"Who did this to you, honey? Do you know?"

Remembering Harriet was on the ASD spectrum and had difficulties talking to people, she reached for her phone. Harriet needed her family and professionals now to find out what had happened to this poor broken girl.

"Tttttttt," she whispered to Mallory.

"What sweetie?"

"Ttthhhhhomas."

She could hardly hear her, and Mallory was sure she hadn't said what it sounded like.

"What?" she asked again, feeling the color draining from her face. "Thomas? Thomas did this to you?"

Harriet squeezed her eyes shut, seemingly hearing his name out loud was more than she could handle, and nodded.

"Oh shit," said Mallory, anxiety clawing through her stomach as she began to call 911.

"What's happening here?"

Mallory spun around to see Susan.

"Oh! Susan! We found…"

Feeling the stab of a needle, she looked at Susan, confused.

And everything went black…

CHAPTER SEVENTEEN

Standing outside his house, looking through the window to his living room, he could not believe what he was seeing.

How in the hell had the girl escaped? He was always so careful.

He needed to get his stupid ass sons out of the house now. If not, he would have to start Plan B, and Susan would not be happy with Plan B.

She loved her boys; she had always felt more emotion than he did. He only tolerated them. Although he had seen potential in his middle child, he knew it was too late for Aiden now.

How would he know text messages could be read without the damn phones?

Running towards the main paddock, he knew he needed to create a diversion before that little bitch spoke to them. Or even worse, they call the fucking pigs.

"Susan, I've found the girl. Get back in the house, and I'll be there. Once I've gotten the boys out of the fucking way," he barked into his phone.

***

Mallory struggled to open her eyes, each attempt leaving her head spinning and the overwhelming urge to be sick. Wondering what the hell she had drunk to deserve such a mighty hangover, swallowing down the nausea, she tried again.

"Oh fuck," she whispered to herself, her last memory slapping her in the face.

Thomas.

Thomas and Susan!

"Oh fuck," she said again, panic now surging through her body, causing her eyes to whip open straight into reality.

She was naked and restrained. Wriggling her limbs to free herself, she realized they had strapped her legs into stirrups, causing them to spread, leaving the junction of her thighs completely on show. Her wrists bound with a cable tie, and around her neck was a thick dog collar, fastened tight enough to apply pressure on her windpipe. A long piece of chain attached the collar to a pole on the ceiling.

Oh shit! What happened to Harriet? Mallory frantically looked around the room for the poor girl. She hadn't realized she was crying until her tears blinded her. Breathing hard, she tried to calm herself down. She needed to assess where she was and if she could free herself. Trying not to have a full-blown meltdown, she looked around the room.

The first thing she noticed was all the sex toys hanging up on one side of the room. Lots of dildos and whips, and an electrocution device next to a cattle prod. Swallowing hard, she desperately tried not to cry anymore when she spotted a wooden coffin at the end of the room with a blood trail on the floor leading to where she sat.

Turning her head away, she observed what was on the other side of the room. There was a toilet in the corner, and a mattress on the floor. Mallory winced and looked at the walls to an enormous map of Portland and the surrounding areas, including Lake Anwar, with little black pins dotted all around. She gasped, guessing they signified the areas where other bodies had been hidden.

Looking at the rest of the wall, which was decorated with what must have been a hundred photos of women, naked and tied up, clearly scared and in lots of pain. Horrified, Mallory couldn't believe what she was seeing. There were so many of them! How long had they been killing for?

Telling herself she would definitely be up for a Pulitzer Prize if she got out of this alive. She tried pulling the chain which connected her to the ceiling; she had no chance of getting out that way, and they had secured the dog collar on with a little padlock.

"How in the hell did Harriet escape?" she asked her reflection, looking up at the mirror directly above her.

Suddenly, the sound of padlocks unlocking came from the only door in the room. Her breathing becoming heavier and quicker with the realization that they were coming back.

Susan walked in first, with Thomas carrying Harriet like a rag doll.

"Ah sweetheart, you're awake," Susan said, smiling. "Bet you'd wish you never stuck your nose in where it didn't belong."

Thomas walked over to the mattress on the floor, dumping an unconscious Harriet on there.

"I'll deal with you later," he growled and walked over to where Mallory sat.

She tried desperately to cringe away from his gaze while he stood, studying her vagina. But there was nowhere she could hide away from him.

"So, another one of my sons got their piece of the pussy first." He nodded in appreciation. "I hope you will behave better than the last one. That bitch was a screamer. She irritated the fuck out of me."

"Where is she now?" Susan asked, pouting. "I was enjoying her."

"In the coffin. I'll sort her out for the dogs' chow later."

Mallory felt sick with the realization. These psychopaths had been feeding his dogs the organs of his victims.

Walking over to the coffin, Susan lifted the lid. Mallory couldn't help but look at the dead body of Freya James. Her dead white eyes, wide open and a plastic pipe imbedded down her throat. Susan stroked Freya's cold, stiff breasts and sighed in disappointment.

"It's a shame you've gotten yourself into this mess, Mallory," Thomas said. "Your dad really is my oldest, best friend."

"Let me go to him, then. Please let me go. I promise I won't say anything. Susan is right. None of this is my business, so let me go and I'll promise___."

"Just shut the fuck up, Mallory. We both know that isn't possible now. Not now you've seen my playpen. And now, after all of this drama, we are short of toys to play with."

Mallory cried again. "Please, think of my dad. It will break him if anything happens to me. He's your best friend, remember? You know he loves me. Please let me go home to him."

Thomas nodded his head and looked at Susan regretfully. "It really is tragic that my old college buddy will go through this twice. But unfortunately, we have no choice again."

"Again? What do you mean again?"

Thomas began to whistle, searching the pictures on the wall. Mallory's breath caught in her throat. She couldn't breathe.

He stopped looking and pointed.

Mallory let out her breath with an ear-piercing scream. Her world exploding around her.

Her mother was in the photo.

She didn't think she could ever stop screaming. Before she could take a breath, Susan came rushing forwards. Smashing her fists into Mallory's face.

"Shut the fuck up! Get the fucking gag, Tom!" Susan shouted, before raining more punches down on Mallory.

Everything went black.

***

Opening her bruised, swollen eyes, Mallory wished she hadn't woken up when observing the horrific sight in front of her.

Thomas had laid Freya onto a big plastic sheeting, and was rummaging through her dead body like it was some kind of sick treasure chest, randomly throwing organs into a bucket.

She wanted to shout at him, call him a sick fuck and to leave Freya's body alone, but they had fitted her with a ball gag. Looking at him with pure hatred, she wanted to scream all the most offensive words she could think of.

He had killed her mother.

He had taken her beautiful mother away from them. And all of this time Mallory had hated her. For years, she had blamed herself for her mom leaving them. But this bastard had put a ball gag in her mouth.

She would have to wait to tell him she was going to kill him.

"Good. You're awake again. Not looking so pretty this time though," said Thomas, standing up from the monstrous act of defiling Freya's body, and walked over to Mallory.

"Bet you have lots of questions, don't ya? Well, I'll explain it to you like I do to all my new toys." He pulled a chair over and sat, wiping his hands with paper towels.

"You have been taken by force, and we will keep you by force. There's nothing you can say that will convince me to let you go. I have been doing this for a long time now, and not even you can persuade me otherwise. It is a real shame you are Will's daughter, especially because I took your momma. And now I see my oldest son has gone soft on you too, but that means fuck all here."

Mallory could feel angry and frustrated tears burning her eyes again. Her mouth had been her only defense, and now they had taken that away from her too.

"Susan and I have had this playpen for years. We like to keep one or two toys around to satisfy our particular needs," he told her matter-of-factly. "Susan is fortunate. She can get off at any time, but she likes to be a little sadistic with a toy once in a while, when someone catches her eye. Like Freya did, then I will take them for her." He smiled like he believed he was being a good husband.

"But in my case, I can't get off with a girl, unless I hurt her first. That's basically the reason I play like I do. And the reason you are going to be subjected to a certain amount of pain. You should feel lucky I am at the age I am, and not the same age as my sons. I was really wild then…"

CHAPTER EIGHTEEN

"Mallory? Where the hell are you?" Noah called, walking out of the living room in search of the girls.

"I'll quickly check upstairs," said Cole, looking just as confused as his brother.

Pulling out his phone, Noah dialed Mallory. Her phone rang inside the living room. Detecting its location under the sofa, Noah held it up with a solemn look. Where in the hell had they gone? Surely the ambulance and police hadn't arrived already and taken Harriet with them?

There's no way Mallory would have left the house without her phone, unless it was kicked under the sofa by accident? Maybe she didn't have the chance to look for it in her rush to stay with Harriet?

But she would have at least left a note, wouldn't she? Noah searched around for a handwritten note, to no avail.

"Nope, not upstairs either," Cole said grimly. "We weren't putting out that damn fire for long! Where could they have gone?"

"I don't have a clue. None of this makes sense. Why would they leave?"

Hearing the front door opening, Noah rushed through, hoping it was Mallory.

"Aiden! What are you doing here?"

"Last time I remember, I lived here. They finally got hold of my friend, who I stayed with that night. Thankfully, he even had me on his home security, so the police had to let me go."

"Well, that's some good news!" said Cole, clapping his older brother on the back. "We found one of the missing girls, driving back from the station."

"What?" Aiden asked, open-mouthed.

"She was beat up pretty badly. We had just got her back to the house, and about to call 911 when Bobby called us away to help put out a damn fire in the stables."

"Shit. Are the horses okay?"

"No casualties, just skittish still," said Cole.

"Thank god," Aiden said, looking relieved.

"When we got back, Mallory and the girl were gone."

"What? They have gone missing again?"

"Seems it," said Noah, planting a hand on his face and rubbing in frustration.

"What about the text messages on your phone?" Cole asked Aiden.

"They finally believed I lost my phone. Security footage doesn't lie. But someone who knew I was seeing Freya must have taken it."

The three brothers looked at each other somberly.

***

Mallory struggled for breath when another bucket of icy cold water hit her.

"It's time to play Mallory."

Blinking the water out from her eyes, she focused on Thomas's face, standing in front of her, between her stretched out legs. Shaking her head, she noticed he was holding a cattle prod.

"No, no, no," she tried to say.

"Sorry, what? You really shouldn't talk with your mouth full, Mallory. It's rude." Thomas sniggered.

"So now you will to be punished." Twisting the dial, he gently held the stick against the inside of her thigh.

She screamed out with shock, when the sharp electric bolts ran through her body, leaving her leg feeling on fire.

He removed the prod and smiled at her seared flesh, leaning closer and inhaling deeply.

He rubbed the bulge which was growing in his pants.

Crying, and trying her hardest to kill Thomas with her hate-filled stare, Mallory couldn't believe this monster was her father's friend. William was filled with compassion and goodness. While this sadistic bastard was filled with depravity and evilness.

"Still got your bad attitude, huh? I am your master. I own you now," he sneered, teasing the cattle prod against her vagina.

Mallory's glare turned into horror. Shaking her head, she begged to him with her eyes.

"That's better." He nodded in approval. "That's how you will look at me from now on."

Running the prod up and away from her most sensitive part. She let out a relieved breath before he wordlessly turned the dial again and placed the prod next to her belly button.

Mallory's stomach muscles tensed with excruciating pain, while the rest of her body received a pulse of sharp, stinging shocks.

Thomas leaned forward and took the ball gag out of her mouth.

"Don't fret about the burns. I'll rub some of my special cream on them," he said, as he undid his pants.

"Please, no." She closed her eyes as he began to masturbate.

"Fucking look at me," he shouted at her. "I want you to tell me who does it better. Me or fucking Noah?"

Hearing Noah's name, she realized she would never see him again. He wouldn't be coming to rescue her. She didn't even know where she was. How could he possibly know?

Knights in shining armor were only in fairy tales, and she was in a horror story.

Not only had Thomas stolen her mother away from her, but he was stealing the chance of her falling in love, too.

"Noah is more of a man than you could ever dream to be," Mallory spat out, surprising herself.

Thomas stopped stroking himself and punched her in her already bruised face.

"That boy has fuck all on me!" he shouted, picking up the cattle prod and positioning it near her vagina.

"See what you think after I've fucked you with..." He paused, staring at her with wide eyes, full of shock.

"This," he said before falling face down on top of her, a knife sticking out of his back.

Gasping, Mallory looked over in amazement to see Harriet, a weak but satisfied smile on her face.

Harriet had summoned what little energy she had left, and dragged herself unnoticed behind Thomas, plunging one of his big knives into his back.

"Harriet! Thank God! How did you do that? You're a clever, clever girl!" Mallory cried, looking at her savior. "Are you able to untie my hands, Harriet? Do you know where the keys are kept?"

Nodding, clearly in shock and in a lot of pain, she staggered over to the drawer where Thomas kept his keys. Harriet had been trapped in the playpen for a long time now, giving her the opportunity to memorize all of Thomas' hiding places. Remembering the shape of each of his keys and knowing what they were all used for.

Asperger's Syndrome may have left Harriet with few social skills, but it had given her the gift of an almost photographic memory.

Picking out the correct key, she forced herself to walk back to where Mallory was sitting, desperately waiting for Harriet to help her.

She stopped in her struggle, frozen in fear when the door to hell smashed open, and Noah came bursting through, pointing a gun and searching the room.

"You sick motherfucker!" he screamed in anger seeing Mallory tied to the chair with his father laying on top of her.

Rushing over, Noah grabbed Thomas by the hair on the back of his head and threw him to the floor. Without a moment's hesitation, he aimed and fired his gun, putting a single bullet into Thomas's chest, his anger overcoming him as he spat on his father's lifeless body before turning back to Mallory.

"You have no idea how pleased I am to see you," Mallory said smiling. Then burst hysterically into tears.

"Oh baby, baby," he soothed, wrapping his arms around her gently, making her feel safe.

"I've got you now."

"Where's Freya?" Aiden demanded.

Mallory looked sorrowfully over at Aiden, who was looking around the room in horrified disgust.

"I'm so sorry, Aiden," Mallory paused, eyes streaming with tears. "It was too late."

"Here Noah, Harriet has the keys," Cole said, looking like he was going to be sick at any moment.

"How did you know? How did you find us?" Mallory asked Noah, who was unlocking her restraints.

"We realized whoever was doing this must have known Aiden was seeing Freya," Noah said, looking worryingly over at Aiden.

"Then when you both went missing from the house, it didn't take too long for us to figure out it was Thomas. I always knew he was a bastard. I just didn't know how much of a sick one he was."

"It wasn't just Thomas..." Mallory paused, the three brothers looking at her in suspense.

"And Susan. Susan was in on it too."

"WHAT?" the three brothers shouted at the same time. Clearly shocked, their mother was capable of such horror.

"My mother was part of this sickness too?" Aiden asked. His face turning red, his eyes getting darker.

"Yes. I'm sorry. She did this to my face."

"Our mom and dad killed my fucking girlfriend," he growled, looking at each of his brothers before storming out.

"Where are you going?" Cole shouted after him.

Aiden, swiftly untying and mounting his horse, glanced back in Cole's direction, his eyes now stone cold.

"To find her."

CHAPTER NINETEEN

The closer Aiden got to the house, the more enraged he became.

He couldn't believe his parents were the killers. Couldn't comprehend how they had blinded them for so long to who they really were.

Jumping down from his horse, he tied Red to their garden fence post. Let him eat the bitch's flowers!

Walking through the back door, he didn't have to look far for his mother. Susan was in the kitchen, casually fixing herself a Mojito.

He couldn't believe his eyes, but he could feel his loss of self-control.

"What the fuck are you doing?"

"Aiden!" said Susan, looking shocked.

"Did you really think we wouldn't find out what sick fucks you both fucking are?"

"What do you mean?" Susan asked, looking around nervously. She picked up the ice-pick she had been using to fix her drink. Holding it with the sharp point hidden from Aiden's view behind her forearm.

"How could you? How could you kill all of those women? How the fuck could you kill my fucking girlfriend?"

"I don't know what you're talking about!" she said, pushing herself away from the worktop and walking around the kitchen table.

"Just stop lying! It's over. We've found Mallory and the girl. Dad was with them."

"You found them? Aiden. You know I could never hurt you. Where is your father now? It was his secret, not mine."

"You are not my mother! You are not who I thought you were. You're an evil fucking whore! A fucking monster!"

"WHERE IS YOUR FATHER?"

Staring at his mother, with a satisfied smirk, "He's fucking dead."

"NOOOO." Screaming in fury, Susan lunged at Aiden, aiming the ice-pick at his chest.

Fighting his mother off, he squeezed her hand until she dropped her weapon.

He grabbed the pick. An enraged Susan began slapping and punching his chest.

Trying to shake her off, they fell to the floor.

On top, and with the pick still in his hand, Aiden struggled to hold Susan's arms down while she was desperately trying to claw at his face.

As they fought, the pick plunged into Susan's neck...

... Just as Elijah entered the house, witnessing Aiden stabbing his mother.

Following his training, he aimed and fired.

***

The first breath Mallory took out of the playpen felt like her very first. It was the sweetest air she had ever inhaled. The adrenaline rushing through her made her visibly shake, causing Noah to hold her tighter.

"It's all over, sweetheart. I've got you."

Cole carried Harriet behind them, leaving their father dead in his own torture room.

"I'll call Jamie now," Cole said, after helping Harriet get into Thomas's truck.

"Yes! Make sure you do it this time," said Noah, as he strapped Mallory in the back seat as gently as he could, and kissed her on the head.

"WHAT?"

Noah groaned, hearing Cole shouting down the phone. Closing the truck door, he looked at his youngest brother questioningly.

"The police are already at the house."

"Well, that's good. But they're in the wrong fucking place!"

They were at the Rileys' first home they had lived in on the ranch land, before they had built the big farmhouse and stables.

Thomas had turned the first stable he had owned into his room of depravity.

"It's not Aiden! It was my parents!" Cole spoke down the phone, alarmingly.

"Oh, shit!" Noah said, starting the truck and hightailing them home, while Cole gave Jamie the correct location.

✳✳✳

Noah parked the truck as close as he could. The emergency services were surrounding the ranch house. He got out and grabbed a paramedic.

Swiftly, they removed Mallory and Harriet from the car and into the ambulance.

Feeling satisfied they were finally receiving the medical attention they needed, Noah walked over to join Cole, standing outside the front of the house.

"Where is Aiden?" asked Cole, looking around.

Spotting Elijah smoking a cigarette, Noah frowned. The rare times he knew of his friend smoking, was when things were bad.

"Eli!" Noah shouted. "We got the girls!"

Elijah threw down his smoke and walked over to his best friend.

"Where did you find them?"

"Locked in our old stables, the far side of the ranch. Where's Aiden?"

"I have some bad news, Noah. I got here too late; Aiden was already attacking your mom when I arrived. I'm so sorry Noah, Cole. She didn't make it."

"Fucking good. Because she wouldn't have made it if I had got my hands on her first either."

Elijah looked at him, shocked.

"What the fuck, man?"

"It was her Eli! All along. It was both my fucking parents who have been taking the women and subjecting them to god knows what."

"What do you mean?"

"Thomas and Susan are the killers," Noah told him grimly.

"No…" Elijah whispered, his expression going from confused to horrified.

"Yes. Thank God we found Mallory and Harriet. Thomas was already dead when we got there. Harriet managed to take him by surprise. I shot the bastard to make sure."

Elijah didn't answer him, seeming unable to find his words.

"Eli, where's Aiden? Didn't he tell you?"

"I am so sorry, Noah. He stabbed your mother. I thought he was the killer."

"Where is my brother, Eli?"

"I'm sorry Noah. He's dead. I shot him. I was trying to save the wrong person."

Noah felt the ground underneath him spin.

No, not Aiden. Not his brother.

Choking back a sob, he looked over at Cole, who had fallen to the ground on his knees.

Elijah's radio went off, he frowned as he stepped away from them.

Digging his fingers in his hair, Noah realised he was crying when his face was wet, and his vision blurry. Memories and images of Aiden flashing through his mind, seemingly all at once.

Feeling an arm around his shoulders, he blinked back his tears to see Elijah holding a very grim expression.

"Noah? I need to speak to you. We have just searched the area; we found the torture room. But there's no Thomas."

Noah felt himself join his brother on the floor.

CHAPTER TWENTY

Watching the casket getting lowered into the ground was a surreal experience. The sun was shining brightly, and the birds were still singing in the trees, bringing the reality of life going on, even after you die.

Holding her father's hand, Mallory gently squeezed Noah's with her other, desperately trying to give him some kind of comfort amongst the small crowd of people who were paying their last respects to Aiden Riley.

Looking around the sad faces of the gloomy ceremony, Mallory couldn't help but think this could easily have been her funeral, if it hadn't been for Harriet.

Cole stood next to Jamie, looking handsome and solemn. Unrecognizable from the happy, go-lucky man she had first met, which seemed a lifetime ago.

Bobby stood nearby, wiping away silent tears. Apart from the Riley brothers, Bobby had been the closest to Aiden, working with him every day. Bobby had been such a pillar for the Rileys, taking over the ranch duties, and hiring more help. The boys hadn't yet decided what they were going to do with

Elm-Green Farm, but for now, they could trust Bobby to keep things running smoothly.

As the mourners trailed away, Mallory let out a sigh of relief. She had little time left before leaving, and she wanted to spend the last few hours alone with Noah.

Feeling Noah tense again, Mallory looked to see Elijah walking towards them.

"Noah," he said, looking sorrowfully at his best friend, and then to Cole.

"Cole. I just want you both to know, I have handed in my badge."

"What? I know this is eating you up, man. But don't throw your career away!" said Cole.

"I've left the force to focus on finding Thomas. I promise you both, over your brother's grave, I will find him. I will not stop searching until I have brought him back and bring him the justice he deserves."

Noah didn't respond, he just looked at Elijah. If Mallory still hadn't been holding his hand, she would have thought Noah hadn't heard him. But she could feel him tighten.

"I will never have the words to tell you how sorry I am. And I will not stop until I have redeemed myself."

Nodding to Cole, and looking full of remorse at Noah, Elijah walked away.

"Eli," Noah said, causing Elijah to turn around.

"When you find him, tell me. I want to be the first to know where he is."

Nodding, Elijah walked away.

✳✳✳

Mallory walked William to his car, and gave her father a big hug.

As soon as William had heard, he had come straight away. She had never seen her dad this angry before; it hurt her heart to see him so full of guilt. It wasn't every day you found out your lifelong friend was a sadistic predator, who had killed the love of your life, and tortured your only daughter.

"I won't be too far behind you, Daddy." She smiled.

Giving Mallory a long look, William kissed her on the head.

"Okay Mally, drive carefully. Just call if you need me to turn back. For anything," William added. Mallory guessed it was going to take some time for William to stop being overprotective of her. He had nearly lost her to his best friend, after all.

Starting the engine, he waved one last time, and drove down the ranch's long drive.

Walking back into the house, Cole was waiting.

"You need me to help you with your bags, Mal?"

"Please. That would be great." She smiled, remembering back to when they had first met. "Is the elevator still not working?" she teased.

Cole sniffed. "No, we do apologize." Then whispered, "I will totally understand, if you leave us a one-star review."

Laughing, she followed Cole back up the stairs. It was only a week before he would leave for college, and Noah back to base. Mallory couldn't imagine the house being empty.

Walking into her room, she looked around, checking she had gathered all of her things together.

"So, I notice you have been seeing Jamie a lot more?"

"He's been great," said Cole, blushing slightly. "He might even be the real deal, you know."

"Good. I'm happy for you, Cole. You look so sweet together."

"Thanks, Mal," he said, grabbing a bag in each hand. "At least I never had to come out to the parents. Always a positive huh?" then noticing her reaction. "Too soon?" He grinned.

"Yes. Too soon." She smiled, following him out of the room and closing her door for the last time.

It relieved her to see Cole still had his spark. She hoped it wouldn't be too long before it came back to his eyes.

After they had finished packing her car, Cole gave her a hug.

"I'm really going to miss you," he said, "But something tells me it will not be for long."

"Where is he?" she asked, breathing in deeply.

"The stables."

Heading towards the stables with a heavy heart, Mallory thought back to the first time she had met the horses. Not only had she come for a story, but she had also come, craving for excitement. Boy, had she gotten more than she could have dreamed of!

She would miss the ranch, but she was looking forward to going home and living the mundane with her father… Just for a little while.

Spotting Noah leaning on the main paddocks' fence, she walked over and stood next to him, silently watching Red, Aiden's horse, galloping around the field.

Mimicking his position, she leaned on the fence. "Hey."

"Hey," he said, turning to her with a small, sad smile. "You all ready to leave?"

"Yep."

Stepping away from the fence, he pulled her closer to him, holding her in his arms.

"I'm going to miss you," she whispered, "so much."

Noah tilted her face upward, meeting her lips with his own, telling her what he wanted to say with his kiss.

"If you wanted me to, I could always stop in Sacramento on my next leave?"

Looking into his eyes, and seeing his uncertainty, Mallory pushed herself up and kissed him again.

"I would really love that, Noah." Telling him with her eyes what she was too scared to say in words.

It was too soon for both of them to declare their love for one another. They had experienced a life-changing ordeal, and they needed the time to sort through their feelings.

Walking slowly back to her car hand in hand, Noah opened the driver's door for her, grabbing her before she got in and giving her a last lingering kiss.

"I am so happy to have met you Mallory. William's daughter, from Sacramento."

Smiling at the memory, she could feel her eyes tearing. Wiping them away, he kissed her on the nose, and walked away, back toward the stables. Not wanting to see her drive away.

Getting into her little car, Mallory put on her sunglasses, hiding the last faint bruises on her face. Turning on her GPS, she programmed the settings for home.

Obi-Wan Kenobi's wise words spoke to her. "You want to go home and rethink your life."

"Well, thanks Obi-Wan. But I don't think I'll be needing your Jedi mind tricks to do that!"

Buckling her seatbelt, Mallory turned on the ignition.

"You ready to go home?" she said, looking down at little Hercules, sitting and wagging his tail on the passenger seat.

"Well, come on then." She smiled and drove out of the ranch, setting off down the long tree-lined driveway for the last time with her adopted companion, paws on the door, looking out of the window and barking at the horses in the distant field.

EPILOGUE

Four months later…

Sitting in the dark, Elijah pressed eject on his computer drive, removed the disc and placed it on the pile he had already seen.

Thanks to Jamie, who had 'borrowed' the box filled with films they had recovered from Thomas's lair. The collection consisted of extreme pornography and BDSM 'snuff' films. At least he didn't need to worry about the films' authenticity, as most snuff films showing 'actual murders' were faked. But unfortunately, he knew these were the real deal.

After checking the Rileys' financial records, they had discovered a high number of international transactions, mainly from Australia and the Philippines. They had guessed correctly; Thomas and Susan had been making snuff movies and selling them to a ring of sexual predators.

He was hoping to see something that would give him some idea to where the sick bastard could have run away to, knowing it would be in anyone's best interest to help hide Thomas away, if he had any damning information against them.

Putting in a new disc, he opened himself another beer, needing the liquid courage, while waiting for it to load. Elijah wouldn't be surprised if these disgusting images gave him nightmares tonight.

Wincing, he rubbed his face as another poor victim lay in Thomas's special chair. Breaking out in a sweat, he skipped the frames filled with torture. He couldn't stand to watch another poor woman become a bloody victim to Thomas's tools.

Lighting another cigarette, he promised himself he would give up his dangerous habit when he had finally made good his pledge to his best friend.

He had hit so many dead ends, regarding sightings and help from the public. Thomas's last known whereabouts had been Mexico, but he had unfortunately moved on by the time Elijah had gotten there. This box felt like his last hope of tracking Thomas down.

Swapping the disc for another, and then another, feeling his soul becoming darker with each clip, Elijah was losing hope. They all seemed to be filmed at the Rileys' ranch, but he was hoping to see something which had not been recorded in Thomas's torture room.

As the evening went on, and he had smoked a full pack of Marlboros, and drank his last beer, he put his hand in the box, feeling for another disc. Not finding anything, Elijah stood up and was about to admit defeat when he noticed one lying flat in the corner.

Looking toward the ceiling, he took a deep breath and inserted the disc.

"Please, for the love of God," he said to his empty study, as the screen went black.

The sound of a woman screaming came from his computer speakers, making him grimace. Low lighting flashed up on the screen, showing a young woman tied with her hands above her head. Elijah looked closer at the screen, realizing this video had not been filmed in Thomas's torture stables, but what looked to be in a warehouse. Finally, he had found something that could be useful in his search.

Scanning the screen, his attention was immediately directed to the stack of storages boxes in the corner of the room. He clicked on the images, taking a screenshot, to enlarge and enhance the labels, which were on some of the boxes. But the only letters he could make out were PE/WA.

Frowning, he played more of the tape. A man in a leather mask was whipping the poor woman. Elijah swallowed the sickness down when the victim begged for her life, but gasped out loud when a strange sound in the background caught his attention. Skipping back, he recorded the unique audio and reached for his phone, knowing the exact person who could confirm his finding.

"Cole? I need you to listen to something for me."

"Christ man! Do you know what time it is? Pretty positive it's not my wakey time."

"Just listen. It's important. Can you tell me what animal this is?"

"Have you been taking drugs, Eli?"

"What? No! Just hear me out."

Holding the phone next to the computer speakers, he pressed play. Pretty certain he was correct, but needing to know from an animal expert before taking his next big step. Knowing Cole was at veterinary school, he trusted Cole's knowledge on the subject.

"Well?" he asked down the phone.

"It's obviously a kookaburra."

"How sure are you?"

"One hundred and ten percent. Why? What do I win?"

"Hopefully, my redemption," Elijah said before hanging up the call.

Leaning back in his chair, his mind buzzing, Elijah knew where he was going.

Perth, Western Australia.

"Gotcha."

To be continued in book two, Pursuing Redemption.

ACKNOWLEDGMENTS

I would like to thank these special people for helping me fulfil my dream of writing and publishing
Missing in Portland.

Aubrey Joy- Thank you so much for your patience and my cover design!

Sally Dabb- Thank you for your invaluable help in correcting my manuscript, and helping with my grammar skills. (Which I know you love to do!)

Charlotte Smith- My final eyes. Forever grateful!

David Allen- My number one test bunny! I always knew if you enjoyed my story, I was on to a winner!

Rebecca Dabb- I hope this had enough gory bits in for you!

Brogan Weston- I will always miss our garden chats and 'spit balling'. Hurry home soon!

Mia Hill- Thank you for your madness! You have given me so many great ideas for future projects.

Jennifer Weston- Thank you for reading my story, and for your feedback.

Matt Cowell- Thank you for all of your feedback. It was always really helpful, and never failed to make me smile!

Jason Ferdinando- My first eyes! Thank you so much for directing me on the correct path.

Joanna Ferdinando- Thank you for reading, your opinion is always important to me.

Lindsey Thorpe- Thank you so much for reading and for your feedback. I hope I never give you nightmares!

Dark Raven Edits- Thank you for your suggestions.

Pauline Allen - You can read this story Mum… Just not the parts in italics!!!

Kenny Dabb - Last, but no way in the least! Thank you, my love… Ready for the next chapter?

And a big thank you to all of my family and friends for their continued support.

THANK YOU FOR READING!

Please add a review on Amazon and let me know what
you thought!

Amazon reviews are extremely helpful for authors, thank you
for taking the time to support my work.

Don't forget to share your review on social media with the
hashtag #MissinginPortland and encourage others to read the
story too!

Don't Forget To Sign Up For The Authors Page!

For special offers, giveaways, bonus content and updates from the author on new releases!

https://clkenny.wixite.com/clkenny
facebook.com/CL-kenny-100487098794059

Printed in Great Britain
by Amazon